RANDOM HOUSE

LARGE PRINT

ALSO BY HARUKI MURAKAMI
AVAILABLE FROM RANDOM HOUSE LARGE PRINT

Killing Commendatore

FIRST PERSON SINGULAR

FIRST PERSON

STORIES

HARUKI

TRANSLATED FROM THE
JAPANESE BY PHILIP GABRIEL

SINGULAR

MURAKAMI

RANDOM HOUSE
LARGE PRINT

Published in the United States of America by Random House Large Print in association with Alfred A. Knopf, a division of Penguin Random House LLC, New York. Originally published in Japan as **Ichininsho Tansu** by Bungei Shunju Ltd., Tokyo, in 2020. Copyright © 2020 by Haruki Murakami.

Some stories first appeared in the following publications: "Cream" first appeared in **The New Yorker** (January 2019), "On a Stone Pillow" first appeared in **Freeman's** (October 2020), "Charlie Parker Plays Bossa Nova" first appeared in **Granta** (August 2019), "With the Beatles" first appeared in **The New Yorker** (February 2020), and "Confessions of a Shinagawa Monkey" first appeared in **The New Yorker** (June 2020).

Front-of-cover photograph by Brent Landreth/Alamy
Spine-of-cover photograph by Hum Images/Alamy
Cover design by Chip Kidd
Title page photograph by Ulana Switucha / Alamy

The Library of Congress has established a
Cataloging-in-Publication record for this title.

ISBN: 978-0-593-39654-4

www.penguinrandomhouse.com/large-print-format-books

FIRST LARGE PRINT EDITION

Printed in the United States of America

10 9 8 7 6 5 4 3 2 1

This Large Print edition published in accord
with the standards of the N.A.V.H.

CONTENTS

CREAM

So I'm telling a younger friend of mine about a strange incident that took place back when I was eighteen. I don't recall exactly why I brought it up. It just happened to come up as we were talking. I mean, it was something that happened long ago. Ancient history. On top of which, I was never able to reach any conclusion about it.

"I'd already graduated from high school then, but wasn't in college yet," I explained. "I was what's called an academic **ronin**, a student who fails the university entrance exam and is waiting to try again. Things felt kind of up in the air," I went on, "but that didn't bother me much. I knew that I could get into a halfway-decent private college if I wanted to. But my parents had insisted that I try for a national university, so I took the exam, knowing all along that it'd be a bust. And, sure enough, I failed. The national university exam back then had a mandatory math section, and I had zero interest in calculus. I spent the next year basically killing time, as if I were creating an alibi. Instead of attending cram school to prepare to retake the exam, I hung out at the local library, plowing my way through thick novels. My parents must have assumed that I was studying there. But, hey, that's life. I found it a lot more enjoyable to read all of Balzac than to delve into the principles of calculus."

At the beginning of October that year,

I received an invitation to a piano recital from a girl who'd been a year behind me in school and had taken piano lessons from the same teacher as I had. Once, the two of us had played a short four-hands piano piece by Mozart. When I turned sixteen, though, I'd stopped taking lessons, and I hadn't seen her after that. So I couldn't figure out why she'd sent me this invitation. Was she interested in me? No way. She was attractive, for sure, though not my type in terms of looks; she was always fashionably dressed and attended an expensive private girls' school. Not at all the kind to fall for a bland, run-of-the-mill guy like me.

When we played that piece together, she gave me a sour look every time I hit a wrong note. She was a better pianist than I was, and I tended to get overly tense, so when the two of us sat side by side and played I bungled a lot of notes. My elbow bumped against hers a few times as well. It wasn't such a difficult piece, and, moreover, I had the easier part. Each time I blew it, she had this "Give me a break" expression on her face. And she'd click her tongue—not loudly, but loud enough that I could catch it. I can still hear that sound, even now. That sound may even have had something to do with my decision to give up the piano.

At any rate, my relationship with her was simply that we happened to study in the same piano school. We'd exchange hellos if we ran into each other there, but I have no memory of our ever sharing anything personal. So suddenly receiving an invitation to her recital (not a solo recital, but a group recital with three pianists) took me completely by surprise—in fact, had me baffled. But one thing I had in abundance that year was time, so I sent off the reply postcard, saying that I would attend. One reason I did this was that I was curious to find out what lay behind the invitation—if, indeed, there was a motive. Why, after all this time, send me an unexpected invitation? Maybe she had become much more skilled as a pianist and wanted to show me that. Or perhaps there was something personal that she wished to convey to me. In other words, I was still figuring out how best to use my sense of curiosity, and banging my head against all kinds of things in the process.

The recital hall was at the top of one of the mountains in Kobe. I took the Hankyu train line as close as I could, then boarded a bus that made its way up a steep, winding road. I got off at a stop near the very top, and after a short walk arrived at the modest-sized concert venue, which was owned and managed by an enormous business conglomerate. I hadn't known that there was a concert hall here, in such an inconvenient spot, at the top of a mountain, in a quiet, upscale residential neighborhood. As you can imagine, there were plenty of things in the world that I didn't know about.

I'd felt that I should bring something to show my appreciation for having been invited, so at a florist's near the train station I had selected a bunch of flowers that seemed to fit the occasion and had them wrapped as a bouquet. The bus had shown up just then, and I'd hopped aboard. It was a chilly Sunday afternoon. The sky was covered with thick gray clouds, and it looked as though a cold rain might start at any minute. There was no wind, though. I was wearing a thin, plain sweater under a gray herringbone jacket with a touch of blue, and I had a canvas bag slung across my shoulder. The jacket was too new, the bag too old and worn out. And in my hands was this gaudy bouquet of red flowers wrapped in cellophane. When I got on the bus decked out like that, the other passengers kept glancing at me. Or maybe it just seemed as if they did. I could feel my cheeks turning red. Back then, I blushed at the slightest provocation. And the redness took forever to go away.

"Why in the world am I here?" I asked myself as I sat hunched over in my seat, cooling my flushed cheeks with my palms. I didn't particularly want to see this girl, or hear the piano recital, so why was I spending all my allowance on a bouquet, and traveling all the way to the top of a mountain on a dreary Sunday afternoon in November? Something must have been wrong with me when I dropped the reply postcard in the mailbox.

The higher up the mountain we went, the fewer passengers there were on the bus, and by the time we arrived at my stop only the driver and I were left. I got off the bus and followed the directions on the invitation up a gently sloping street. Each time I turned a corner, the harbor came briefly into view and then disappeared again. The overcast sky was a dull color, as if blanketed with lead. There were a lot of cranes down in the harbor, jutting into the air like the antennae of some ungainly creatures that had crawled out of the ocean.

The houses near the top of the slope were large and luxurious, with massive stone walls, impressive front gates, and two-car garages. The azalea hedges were all neatly trimmed. I heard what sounded like a huge dog barking somewhere. It barked loudly three times, and then, as if someone had scolded it severely, it abruptly stopped, and all around became quiet.

AS I FOLLOWED the simple map on the invitation, I was struck by a vague, disconcerting premonition. Something just wasn't right. First of all, there was the lack of people in the street. Since getting off the bus, I hadn't seen a single pedestrian. Two cars did drive by, but they were on their way down the slope, not up. If a recital was really about to take place here, I would have expected to see more people. But the whole neighborhood was still and silent, as if the dense clouds above had swallowed up all sound.

Had I misunderstood?

I took the invitation out of my jacket pocket to recheck the information. Maybe I'd misread it. I went over it carefully, but I couldn't find anything wrong. I had the right street, the right bus stop, the right date and time. I took a deep breath to calm myself and set off again. The only thing I could do was get to the concert hall and see.

When I finally arrived at the building, the large steel gate was locked tight. A thick chain ran around the gate and was held in place by a heavy padlock. No one else was around. Through a narrow opening in the gate, I could see a fair-sized parking lot, but not a single car was parked there. Weeds had sprouted between the paving stones, and the parking lot looked as if it hadn't been used in quite some time. Despite all that, the large nameplate at the entrance told me that this was indeed the recital hall I was looking for.

I pressed the button on the intercom next to the entrance, but no one responded. I waited a bit, then pressed the button again, but still no answer. I looked at my watch. The recital was supposed to start in fifteen minutes. But there was no sign that the gate would be opened. Paint had peeled off it in spots, and it was starting to rust. I couldn't think of anything else to do, so I pressed the intercom button one more time, holding it down longer, but the result was the same as before—deep silence.

With no idea what to do, I leaned back against the heavy steel gate and stood there for some ten minutes. I had a faint hope that someone else might show up before long. But no one came. There was no sign of any movement, either inside the gate or outside. There was no wind. No birds chirping, no dogs barking. As before, an unbroken blanket of gray cloud lay above.

I finally gave up—what else could I do?—and with heavy steps started back down the street toward the bus stop, totally in the dark about what was going on. The only clear thing about the whole situation was that there wasn't going to be a piano recital or any other event held here today. All I could do was head home, bouquet of red flowers in hand. My mother would doubtless ask, "What're the flowers for?," and I would have to give some plausible answer. I wanted to toss them in the trash can at the station, but they were—for me, at least—kind of expensive to just throw away.

Down the hill a short distance, there was a cozy little park, about the size of a house lot. On the far side of the park, away from the street, was an angled natural rock wall. It was barely a park—it had no water fountain or playground equipment. All that was there was a little arbor, plunked down in the middle. The walls of the arbor were slanted latticework, overgrown with ivy. There were bushes around it, and flat square stepping stones on the ground. It was hard to say what the park's purpose was, but someone was regularly taking care of it; the trees and bushes were smartly clipped, with no weeds or trash around. On the way up the hill, I'd walked right by the park without noticing it.

I went into the park to gather my thoughts and sat down on a bench in the arbor. I felt that I should wait in the area a little longer to see how things developed (for all I knew, people might suddenly appear), and once I sat down I realized how tired I was. It was a strange kind of exhaustion, as though I'd been worn out for quite a while but hadn't noticed it, and only now had it hit me. From the arbor, there was a panoramic view of the harbor. A number of large container ships were docked at the pier. From the top of the mountain, the stacked metal containers looked like nothing more than the small tins you keep on your desk to hold coins or paper clips.

After a while, I heard a man's voice in the distance. Not a natural voice, but one amplified by a loudspeaker. I couldn't catch what was being said, but there was a pronounced pause after each sentence, and the voice spoke precisely, without a trace of emotion, as if trying to convey something extremely important as objectively as possible. It occurred to me that maybe this was a personal message directed at me, and me alone. Someone was going to the trouble of telling me where I'd gone wrong, what it was that I'd overlooked. Not something I would normally have thought, but for some reason it struck me that way. I listened carefully. The voice got steadily louder and easier to understand. It must have been coming from a loudspeaker on the roof of a car that was slowly wending its way up the slope, seemingly in no hurry at all. Finally, I realized what it was: a car broadcasting a Christian message.

"Everyone will die," the voice said in a calm monotone. "Every person will eventually pass away. No one can escape death or the judgment that comes afterward. After death, everyone will be severely judged for his sins."

I sat there on the bench, listening to this message. I found it strange that anyone would do mission outreach in this deserted residential area up on top of a mountain. The people who lived here all owned multiple cars and were affluent. I doubted that they were seeking salvation from sin. Or maybe they were? Income and status might be unrelated to sin and salvation.

"But all those who seek salvation in Jesus Christ and repent of their sins will have their sins forgiven by the Lord. They will escape the fires of Hell. Believe in God, for only those who believe in Him will reach salvation after death and receive eternal life."

I was waiting for the Christian-mission car to appear on the street in front of me and say more about the judgment after death. I think I must have been hoping to hear words spoken in a reassuring, resolute voice, no matter what they were. But the car never showed up. And, at a certain point, the voice began to grow quieter, less distinct, and before long I couldn't hear anything anymore. The car must have turned in another direction, away from where I was. When that car disappeared, I felt as though I'd been abandoned by the world. A sudden thought hit me: Maybe the whole thing was a hoax that the girl had cooked up. This idea—or hunch, I should say—came out of nowhere. For some reason that I couldn't fathom, she'd deliberately given me false information and dragged me out to the top of a remote mountain on a Sunday afternoon. Maybe I had done something that had caused her to form a personal grudge against me. Or maybe, for no special reason, she found me so unpleasant that she couldn't stand it. And she'd sent me an invitation to a nonexistent recital and was now gloating—laughing her head off—seeing (or, rather, imagining) how she'd fooled me and how pathetic and ridiculous I looked.

Okay, but would a person really go to all the trouble of coming up with such a complicated plot in order to harass someone, just out of spite? Even printing up the postcard must have taken some effort. Could someone really be that mean? I couldn't remember a thing I'd ever done to make her hate me that much. But sometimes, without even realizing it, we trample on people's feelings, hurt their pride, make them feel bad. I speculated on the possibility of this not-unthinkable hatred, the misunderstandings that might have taken place, but found nothing convincing. And as I wandered fruitlessly through this maze of emotions, I felt my mind losing its way. Before I knew it, I was having trouble breathing.

This used to happen to me once or twice a year. I think it must have been stress-induced hyperventilation. Something would fluster me, my throat would constrict, and I wouldn't be able to get enough air into my lungs. I'd panic, as if I were being swept under by a rushing current and were about to drown, and my body would freeze. All I could do at those times was crouch down, close my eyes, and patiently wait for my body to return to its usual rhythms. As I got older, I stopped experiencing these symptoms (and, at some point, I stopped blushing so easily, too), but in my teens I was still troubled by these problems.

On the bench in the arbor, I screwed my eyes tightly shut, bent over, and waited to be freed from that blockage. It may have been five minutes, it may have been fifteen. I don't know how long. All the while, I watched as strange patterns appeared and vanished in the dark, and I slowly counted them, trying my best to get my breathing back under control. My heart beat out a ragged tempo in my rib cage, as if a terrified mouse were racing about inside.

I'd been focusing so much on counting that it took some time for me to become aware of the presence of another person. It felt as if someone were in front of me, observing me. Cautiously, ever so slowly, I opened my eyes and raised my head a degree. My heart was still thumping.

Without my noticing, an old man had sat down on the bench across from me and was looking straight at me. It isn't easy for a young man to judge an elderly person's age. To me, they all just looked like old people. Sixty, seventy—what was the difference? They weren't young anymore, that was all. The man was thin, of medium height, and was wearing a bluish-gray wool cardigan, brown corduroy pants, and navy-blue sneakers. It looked as though a considerable amount of time had passed since any of these were new. Not that he appeared shabby or anything. His gray hair was thick and stiff looking, and tufts sprung up above his ears like the wings of birds when they bathe. He wasn't wearing glasses. I didn't know how long he'd been there, but I had the feeling that he'd been observing me for quite some time.

I was sure he was going to say, "Are you all right?," or something like that, since I must have looked as if I were having trouble (and I really was). That was the first thing that sprang to mind when I saw the old man. But he didn't say a thing, didn't ask anything, just gripped a tightly folded black umbrella that he was holding like a cane. The umbrella had an amber-colored wooden handle and looked sturdy enough to serve as a weapon if need be. I assumed that he lived in the neighborhood, since he had nothing else with him.

I sat there trying to calm my breathing, the old man silently watching. His gaze didn't waver for an instant. It made me feel uncomfortable—as if I'd wandered into someone's backyard without permission—and I wanted to get up from the bench and head off to the bus stop as fast as I could. But, for some reason, I couldn't get to my feet. Time passed, and then suddenly the old man spoke.

"A circle with many centers."

I looked up at him. Our eyes met. His forehead was extremely broad, his nose pointed. As sharply pointed as a bird's beak. I couldn't say a thing, so the old man quietly repeated the words: "A circle with many centers."

Naturally, I had no clue what he was trying to say. A thought came to me—that this man had been driving the Christian loudspeaker car. Maybe he'd parked nearby and was taking a break? No, that couldn't be it. His voice was different from the one I'd heard. The loudspeaker voice was a much younger man's. Or perhaps that had been a recording.

"Circles, did you say?" I reluctantly asked. He was older than me, and politeness dictated that I respond.

"There are several centers—no, sometimes an infinite number—and it's a circle with no circumference." The old man frowned as he said this, the wrinkles on his forehead deepening. "Are you able to picture that kind of circle in your mind?"

My mind was still out of commission, but I gave it some thought, just as a courtesy. A circle that has several centers and no circumference. But, think as I might, I couldn't visualize it.

"I don't get it," I said.

The old man silently stared at me. He seemed to be waiting for a better answer.

"I don't think they taught us about that kind of circle in math class," I feebly added.

The old man slowly shook his head. "Of course not. That's to be expected. Because they don't teach you that kind of thing in school. They never teach what's important in school. As you know very well."

As I knew very well? Why would this old man presume that?

"Does that kind of circle really exist?" I asked.

"Of course it does," the old man said, nodding a few times. "That circle does indeed exist. But not everyone can see it, you know."

"Can you see it?"

The old man didn't reply. My question hung awkwardly in the air for a moment, and finally grew hazy and disappeared.

THE OLD MAN spoke again. "Listen, you've got to imagine it with your own power. Use all the wisdom you have and picture it. A circle that has many centers but no circumference. If you put in such an intense effort that you feel like you're sweating blood—that's when it gradually becomes clear what the circle is."

"It sounds difficult," I said.

"Of course it is," the old man said, sounding as if he were spitting out something hard. "There's nothing worth getting in this world that you can get easily." Then, as if starting a new paragraph, he briefly cleared his throat. "But, when you put in that much time and effort, if you do achieve that difficult thing it becomes the cream of your life."

"Cream?"

"In French, they have an expression: **crème de la crème**. Do you know it?"

"I don't," I said. I knew no French.

"The cream of the cream. It means the best of the best. The most important essence of life—that's the **crème de la crème**. Get it? The rest is just boring and worthless."

At the time I didn't really understand what the old man was getting at. **Crème de la crème?**

"Think about it," the old man said. "Close your eyes again, and think it all through. A circle that has many centers but no circumference. Your brain is made to think about difficult things. To help you get to a point where you understand something that you didn't understand at first. You can't be lazy or neglectful. Right now is a critical time. Because this is the period when your brain and your heart form and solidify."

I closed my eyes again and tried to picture that circle. I didn't want to be lazy or neglectful. I tried to think of a circle with many centers but no circumference. But no matter how seriously I thought about what the man was saying, it was impossible for me at that time to grasp the meaning of it. The circles I knew had one center, and a curved circumference connecting points that were equidistant from it. The kind of simple figure you can draw with a compass. Wasn't the kind of circle the old man was talking about the opposite of a circle?

I didn't think that the old man was off, mentally. And I didn't think that he was teasing me. He wanted to convey something important. That much I could get, for some reason. So I tried again to understand, but my mind just spun around and around, making no progress. How could a circle that had many (or perhaps an infinite number of) centers exist as a circle? Was this some advanced philosophical metaphor? I gave up and opened my eyes. I needed more clues.

But the old man wasn't there anymore. I looked all around, but there was no sign of anyone in the park. It was as if he'd never existed. Was I imagining things? No, of course it wasn't some fantasy. He'd been right there in front of me, tightly gripping his umbrella, speaking quietly, posing a strange question, and then he'd left.

I realized that my breathing was back to normal, calm and steady. The rushing current was gone. Here and there, gaps had started to appear in the thick layer of clouds above the harbor. A ray of light had broken through, illuminating the aluminum housing on top of a crane, as if it had been accurately aiming at that one spot. I stared for a long while, transfixed by the almost mythic scene.

The small bouquet of red flowers, wrapped in cellophane, was beside me. Like a kind of proof of all the strange things that had happened to me that day. I debated what to do with it, and ended up leaving it on the bench by the arbor. To me, that seemed the best option. I stood up and headed toward the bus stop where I'd gotten off earlier. The wind had started blowing, scattering the stagnant clouds above.

After I finished telling this story, there was a pause, then my younger friend said, "I don't really get it. What actually happened, then? Was there some intention or principle at work?"

Those very odd circumstances I experienced on top of that mountain in Kobe on a Sunday afternoon in late autumn—following the directions on the invitation to where the recital was supposed to take place, only to discover that the building was deserted—what did it all mean? And why did it happen? That was what my friend was asking. Perfectly natural questions, especially because the story I was telling him didn't reach any conclusion.

"I don't understand it myself, even now," I admitted.

It was permanently unsolved, like some ancient riddle. What took place that day was incomprehensible, inexplicable, and at eighteen it left me bewildered and mystified. So much so that, for a moment, I nearly lost my way.

"But I get the feeling," I said, "that principle or intention wasn't really the issue."

My friend looked confused. "Are you telling me that there's no need to know what it was all about?"

I nodded.

"But if it were me," he said, "I'd be bothered no end. I'd want to know the truth, why something like that happened. If I'd been in your shoes, that is."

"Yeah, of course. Back then, it bothered me, too. A lot. It hurt me, too. But thinking about it later, from a distance, after time had passed, it came to feel insignificant, not worth getting upset about. I felt as though it had nothing at all to do with the cream of life."

"The cream of life," he repeated.

"Things like this happen sometimes in our lives," I told him. "Inexplicable, illogical events that nevertheless are deeply disturbing. I guess we need to not think about them, just close our eyes and get through them. As if we were passing under a huge wave."

My younger friend was quiet for a time, considering that huge wave. He was an experienced surfer, and there were lots of things, serious things, that he had to consider when it came to waves. Finally, he spoke. "But not thinking about anything might also be pretty hard."

"You're right. It might be hard indeed."

There's nothing worth getting in this world that you can get easily, the old man had said, with unshakable conviction, like Pythagoras explaining his theorem.

"About that circle with many centers but no circumference," my friend asked. "Did you ever find an answer?"

"Good question," I said. I slowly shook my head. Had I?

In my life, whenever an inexplicable, illogical, disturbing event takes place (I'm not saying that it happens often, but it has a few times), I always come back to that circle—the circle with many centers but no circumference. And, as I did when I was eighteen, on that arbor bench, I close my eyes and listen to the beating of my heart.

Sometimes I feel that I can sort of grasp what that circle is, but a deeper understanding eludes me. This happens again and again. This circle is, most likely, not a circle with a concrete, actual form but, rather, one that exists only within our minds. That's what I think. When we truly love somebody with all our heart, or feel deep compassion, or have an idealistic sense of how the world should be, or when we discover faith (or something close to faith)—that's when we understand the circle as a given and accept it in our hearts. Admittedly, though, this is nothing more than my own vague attempt to reason it out.

Your brain is made to think about difficult things. To help you get to a point where you understand something that you didn't understand at first. And that becomes the cream of your life. The rest is boring and worthless. That was what the gray-haired old man told me. On a cloudy Sunday afternoon in late autumn, on top of a mountain in Kobe, as I clutched a small bouquet of red flowers.

And even now, whenever something disturbing happens to me, I ponder again that special circle, and **the boring and the worthless**. And the unique cream that must be there, deep inside me.

. . .

ON A STONE PILLOW

'D LIKE TO TELL A STORY about a woman. The thing is, I know next to nothing about her. I can't even remember her name, or her face. And I'm willing to bet she doesn't remember me, either.

When I met her, I was a sophomore in college, and I'm guessing she was in her mid-twenties. We both had part-time jobs at the same place, at the same time. It was totally unplanned, but we ended up spending a night together. And never saw each other again.

At nineteen, I knew nothing about the inner workings of my own heart, let alone the hearts of others. Still, I thought I had a pretty good grasp of how happiness and sadness worked. What I couldn't yet grasp were all the myriad phenomenon that lay in the space between happiness and sadness, how they related to each other. As a result, I often felt anxious and helpless.

That said, I still want to talk about her. What I do know about her is that she wrote tanka poems and had published a book of poetry. I say published, but the book was actually a pamphlet-like volume that barely rose to the level of a self-published book, composed of printed pages bound with string, and a simple cover attached. But several of the poems in her collection were strangely unforgettable. Most of her poems were about love between men and women, or about death. Almost as if to show that love and death were concepts that could not be separated or divided.

You and I
are we really so far apart?
Should I, maybe
have changed trains at Jupiter?

When I press my ear
against the stone pillow
The sound of blood flowing
is absent, absent

"I might yell another man's name when I come. Are you okay with that?" she asked me. We were naked, under the covers.

"I'm okay with that, I guess," I said. I wasn't totally sure, but I thought it probably wouldn't bother me. I mean, it's just a name. Nothing's going to change because of a name.

"I might yell pretty loud."

"Well, that could be a problem," I said hurriedly. The ancient wooden apartment I lived in had walls as thin and flimsy as one of those wafers I used to eat as a kid. It was pretty late at night, and if she really screamed, the people next door would hear it all.

"I'll bite down on a towel, then," she said.

I picked out the cleanest, thickest towel in the bathroom, brought it back, and laid it next to the pillow.

"Is this one okay?"

She bit down on the towel, like a horse testing a new bit. She nodded. The towel passed muster, apparently.

It was totally a chance hookup. I hadn't particularly been hoping we'd get together, and I don't think she had been, either. We'd worked at the same place for a couple of weeks, but since the work we did was a little different, we hardly ever had any chance for a decent conversation. That winter I was washing dishes and helping out in the kitchen of a down-market Italian restaurant near Yotsuya station, and she worked there as a waitress. All the part-timers were college students, except her. Maybe that's why she seemed a bit aloof.

She decided to quit that job in the middle of December, and one day after work, some of the employees went to a nearby **izakaya** for some drinks. I was invited to join them. It wasn't exactly a full-blown farewell party, just us drinking draft beer, having some snacks, chatting about various things. I learned that before she waitressed she'd worked at a small real estate agency and at a bookstore. In all the places she worked, she explained, she never got along with the managers or owners. At the restaurant, she didn't have any arguments with anyone, she explained, but the pay was too low for her to get by for long, so she had to look for another job. Not that she wanted to.

What kind of job do you want to get? someone asked.

"I don't care," she said, rubbing the side of her nose. (Beside her nose there were two small moles, lined up like a constellation.) "I mean, whatever I wind up with isn't going to be all that great anyway."

I lived in Asagaya at the time, and her place was in Koganei. So we rode the high-speed train together on the Chuo line out of Yotsuya. We sat down side by side in the train. It was past eleven p.m., a bitterly cold night, with a biting wind.

Before I'd known it we were in the season where you needed gloves and a muffler. As the train approached Asagaya I stood up, ready to get off, and she looked up at me and said, in a low voice, "If it's okay, would you let me stay at your place tonight?"

"Okay—but how come?"

"It's too far to go all the way back to Koganei."

"I have to warn you, it's a tiny apartment, and a real mess," I said.

"That doesn't bother me in the least," she said, and took the arm of my coat.

So she came to my cramped, crummy place, and we drank some cans of beer. We took our time with the beer, and afterward, like it was a natural next step, she shed her clothes right in front of me. Just like that, she was naked, and snuggled into my futon. Following her lead, I took off my clothes and joined her in bed. I switched off the light, but the glow from the gas stove kept the room fairly bright. In bed we awkwardly warmed each other up. For a while, neither of us said a word. So quickly naked with each other, it was hard to know what to talk about. But as our bodies gradually warmed up, we literally felt the awkwardness loosen up through our skin. It was an oddly intimate sensation.

That's when she asked, "I might yell another man's name when I come. Are you okay with that?"

"Do you love him?" I asked her, after I'd gotten the towel ready.

"I do. A lot," she said. "I love him so, so much. I'm always thinking of him, every minute. But he doesn't love me that much. What I mean is, he has a girlfriend."

"But you're seeing him?"

"Um. He calls me whenever he wants

my body," she said. "Like ordering take-out over the phone."

I had no clue how to respond, so I kept quiet. She traced a figure on my back with her fingertips. Or maybe she was writing something, in cursive.

"He told me that my face is plain but my body is the best."

I didn't think her face was particularly plain, though calling her beautiful was going too far. Looking back on it now, I can't recall what kind of face she had, exactly, or describe it in any detail.

"But if he calls, you go?"

"I love him, so what else can I do?" she said, like nothing could be more natural. "No matter what he says to me, there are just times when I'm dying to have a man make love to me."

I considered this. But back then it was beyond me to imagine what feelings this entailed—for a woman to want a man to make love to her. (And even now, come to think of it, I don't entirely understand it.)

"Loving someone is like having a mental illness that's not covered by health insurance," she said, in a flat tone, like she was reciting something written on the wall.

"I see," I said, moved by her words.

"So it's okay if you think of some other woman instead of me," she said. "Don't you have anybody you like?"

"Yeah, I do."

"So I don't mind if you yell that person's name when you come. It won't bother me at all."

There **was** a girl I liked at the time, but circumstances kept us from getting more deeply involved, and when the moment arrived, I didn't call out her name. The thought crossed my mind, but in the middle of sex it seemed kind of stupid, and I ejaculated inside the woman without a word. She was about to yell a man's name, like she said she would, and I had to hurriedly stuff the towel between her teeth. She had really strong, healthy-looking teeth. Any dentist would be properly impressed. I don't even remember what name she yelled. All I recall is that it was some nothing, run-of-the-mill name, and that I was impressed that such a bland name was, for her, precious and important. A simple name can sometimes really jolt a person's heart.

THE NEXT MORNING, I had an early class where I had to submit a major report in lieu of a midterm, but as you can imagine, I blew it off. (Which led to some huge problems later, but that's another story.) We finally woke up in the late morning, and boiled water for instant coffee, and ate some toast. There were some eggs in the fridge, so I boiled them for us to eat. The sky was clear and cloudless, the morning sunlight dazzling, and I was feeling pretty lazy.

As she munched on buttered toast, she asked me what I was majoring in at college. I'm in the literature department, I said.

Do you want to be a novelist? she asked.

I'm not really planning to, I answered honestly. I had no plans whatsoever at the time of becoming a novelist. I'd never even considered it (though there were plenty of people in my class who'd announced that they were planning to become novelists). With this, she seemed to lose interest in me. Not that she had much interest to begin with. But still.

In the light of day, I could see that her teeth marks were imprinted on the towel, and it struck me as a little bizarre. She must have bitten down on it pretty hard. In the light of day, she seemed out of place. It was hard to believe that this girl—small, bony, with a not-so-great complexion—was the same girl who, the night before, had screamed out passionately in my arms, in the winter moonlight.

"I write tanka poems," she said, out of the blue.

"Tanka?"

"You know tanka, right?"

"Sure," I said. Even someone as naive as me knew that much. "But this is the first time I've met someone who actually writes them."

She gave a happy laugh. "But there are people like that in the world, you know."

"Are you in a poetry club or something?"

"No, it's not like that," she said. She gave a slight shrug. "Tanka are something you write by yourself. Right? It's not like playing basketball."

"What kind of tanka?"

"Do you want to hear some?"

I nodded.

"Really? You're not just saying that?"

"Really," I said.

And that was the truth. I was curious. I mean, what kind of poems would she write, this girl who, a few hours before, had moaned in my arms and yelled another man's name?

She hesitated. "I don't think I can recite any here. It's embarrassing. And it's still morning. But I did publish a kind of collection, so if you really want to read them, I'll send it to you. Could you tell me your full name and address?"

I jotted down my address on a piece of memo paper and handed it to her. She glanced at it, folding it in four, then stuffed it in the pocket of her overcoat. A light green coat that had seen better days. On the rounded collar was a silver broach shaped like a lily of the valley. I remember how it glistened in the sunlight that was streaming in through the south-facing window. I know next to nothing about flowers, but for some reason I've always liked lilies of the valley.

"Thanks for letting me stay over. I truly didn't want to ride back to Koganei on my own," she said as she was leaving my place. "That happens with girls sometimes."

We were both well aware of it then. That we would probably never see each other again. That night she simply didn't want to ride the train all the way back to Koganei—that's all there was to it.

A WEEK LATER, her poetry collection arrived in the mail. Honestly, I really didn't expect her to follow up and send it. I figured she'd totally forgotten about me by the time she got back to her place in Koganei (or perhaps she'd tried to forget me as soon as she could), and never imagined that she'd go to all the trouble to put a copy of the book in an envelope, write my name and address, stick on a stamp, and toss it in a mailbox—maybe even going all the way to the post office, for all I knew. So one morning, when I spied that package in my mail slot in the apartment, it took me by surprise.

The title of the poetry collection was **On a Stone Pillow.** The author was listed as Chiho. It wasn't clear if this was her real name or a pen name. At the restaurant I must have heard her name many times, but I couldn't recall it. No one called her Chiho, though, that much I knew. The collection was in a plain brown business envelope, with no name or return address, and no card or letter included. Just one copy of a thin poetry collection, bound together with white string, silently resting inside. It wasn't some cheap mimeograph, but nicely printed on thick, high-quality paper. I'm guessing the author arranged the pages in order, attached the cardboard cover, and carefully hand-bound each copy using a needle and string to save on bookbinding costs. I tried imagining her doing that sort of work, but couldn't picture it. The number 28 was stamped on the first page. Must have been the twenty-eighth in a limited edition. How many were there altogether? There was no price indicated anywhere. Maybe there never was a price.

I didn't open the poetry collection right away. I left it on top of my desk, casting the occasional glance at the cover. It wasn't that I wasn't interested, it's just I felt that reading a poetry collection someone put together—especially a person who, a week before, has been naked in my arms—required a bit of mental preparation. A sort of respect toward it, I suppose. Finally, that weekend, in the evening, I opened the book. I leaned back against the wall next to the window and read it in the winter twilight. There were forty-two poems contained in the collection. One tanka per page. Not a particularly large number. There was no foreword, no afterword, not even a date of publication. Just printed tanka in straightforward black type on white pages with generous margins.

I certainly wasn't expecting some monumental literary work or anything. Like I said, I was simply curious. What kind of poems would come from a woman who yelled some guy's name in my ear as she bit on a towel? What I found as I read through the collection was that several of the poems really got to me.

Tanka were basically a mystery to me (and still are, even now). So I'm certainly not able to venture an objective opinion about which tanka are considered great, and which ones not so much. But apart from any judgments of literary value, several of the tanka she wrote—eight of them, specifically—struck a chord deep within me.

This one, for instance:

> The present moment
> if it is the present moment
> can only be taken
> as the inescapable present

> In the mountain wind
> a head cut off
> without a word
> June water at the roots of
> a hydrangea

Strangely enough, as I opened the pages of the poetry collection, following the large, black printed words with my eyes and reading them aloud, the girl's body I saw that night came back to my mind, exactly as it was. Not the less-than-impressive figure I saw in the morning light, but the way she was as I held her body, enveloped by smooth skin, in that moonlit night. Her shapely round breasts, the small hard nipples, the sparse pubic hair, her wet vagina. As she reached orgasm, she shut her eyes, bit down hard on the towel, and called out, again and again, another man's name in my ear. The name of a man somewhere, a plain name I can't even recall.

> As I consider that
> we'll never meet again
> I also consider how
> there's no reason that we cannot

Will we meet
or will it simply end like this
drawn by the light
trampled by shadows

I have no idea, of course, whether she's still writing tanka or not. As I said, I don't even know her name, and hardly remember her face at all. What I do remember is the name Chiho on the cover of the collection, her defenseless, supple flesh in the pale winter moonlight shining through the window, and the mini-constellation of two small moles beside her nose.

Perhaps she's not even alive anymore. Sometimes I think that. I can't help but feel that maybe at some point she took her own life. I say this because most of her tanka—or at least most of the ones in that collection—depicted images of death. And for some reason these involved a head being severed with a blade. For her, that style might have been her own way of dying.

> Lost in this incessant
> afternoon downpour
> a nameless ax
> decapitates the twilight

But in a corner of my heart, I'm still wishing she's alive somewhere in this world. Sometimes I'll catch myself, all of sudden, hoping that she's survived, that she's still composing poetry. Why? Why do I take the trouble to think about something like that? There's not one thing that connects my life and hers. Even if, say, we passed each other on a street, or were seated at adjoining tables in a restaurant, I seriously doubt that we would even recognize each other.

Like two straight lines overlapping, we momentarily crossed at a certain point, then went our separate ways.

Many years have passed since then. Strangely enough (or perhaps not so strangely), people age in the blink of an eye. Each and every moment, our bodies are on a one-way journey to collapse and deterioration, unable to turn back the clock. I close my eyes, I open them again, only to realize that in the interim so many things have vanished. Buffeted by the intense midnight winds, these things—some with names, some without—disappear without a trace. All that is left is a faint memory. Even memory, though, can hardly be relied on. Can anyone say for certain what **really** happened to us back then?

If we're blessed, though, a few words might remain by our side. They climb to the top of the hill during the night, crawl into small holes dug to fit the shape of their bodies, stay quite still, and let the stormy winds of time blow past. The dawn finally breaks, the wild wind subsides, and the surviving words quietly peek out from the surface. For the most part they have small voices—they are shy and only have ambiguous ways of expressing themselves. Even so, they are ready to serve as witnesses. As honest, fair witnesses. But in order to create those enduring, long-suffering words, or else to find them and leave them behind, you must sacrifice, unconditionally, your own body, your very own heart. You have to lay down your neck on a cold stone pillow illuminated by the winter moon.

Aside from me, maybe there's not another soul in this world who remembers that girl's poems, let alone someone who can recite them. With the exception of number 28, that slim little self-published book, bound together with string, is now forgotten, dispersed, sucked up somewhere into the benighted darkness between Jupiter and Saturn, vanished forever. Perhaps she herself (assuming she's still alive) can't recall a thing about those poems she wrote back when she was young. Maybe the only the reason I recall some of her poetry even now is because it's linked to memories of her teeth marks on that towel. Maybe that's all it is. I don't know how much meaning or value there is in still remembering all that, in sometimes pulling out that faded copy of the poetry collection from my drawer and reading it again. To tell the truth, I really don't know.

At any rate, those remained. While other words and memories turned to dust and vanished.

Whether you cut it off
or someone else cuts it off
if you put your neck on the stone
   pillow
believe it—you will turn to dust

CHARLIE PARKER

PLAYS BOSSA NOVA

B IRD IS BACK.

How fantastic that sounds! Yes indeed, the Bird you know and love has returned, his powerful wings beating the air. In every corner of this planet—from Novosibirsk to Timbuktu— people are going to gaze up in the sky, spy the shadow of that magnificent bird, and cheer. And the world will be filled once more with brilliant sunlight.

The time is 1963. Years since people last heard the name Charlie

"Bird" Parker. Where is Bird, and what is he up to? Jazz lovers around the world whispered these questions. He can't be dead yet, can he? Because we never heard of him passing away. But you know, someone would say, I haven't heard anything about him still being alive, either.

The last news anyone had heard about Bird was that his patron, Baroness Nica, took him into her mansion, where he battled various ailments. Jazz fans are well aware of Bird's struggles as a junkie. Heroin—that deadly, pure white powder. Rumor had it that on top of his addiction he struggled with acute pneumonia, a variety of internal maladies, the symptoms of diabetes, and ultimately mental illness. Even if he was fortunate enough to survive all these, people thought, he would be so infirmed that he'd never pick up his instrument again. That's how Bird vanished from sight, transforming into a beautiful jazz legend. Around the year 1955.

Fast-forward to the summer of 1963. Charlie Parker picked up his alto sax again to record an album in a recording studio outside of New York. And that album's title is **Charlie Parker Plays Bossa Nova!**

Can you believe it?

You'd better. Because it happened.

It really did.

THIS WAS THE OPENING of a piece I wrote back in college. It was the first time anything I wrote got published, and the first time I got paid a fee for something I'd written, even if it was a pittance.

Naturally, there's no such record titled **Charlie Parker Plays Bossa Nova.** Charlie

Parker passed away on March 12, 1955, and it wasn't until 1962 that bossa nova broke through, spurred on by performances by Stan Getz and others. But **if** Bird had survived until the 1960s, and **if** he got interested in bossa nova, and had performed it . . . That was the setup for the review I wrote about this imaginary record.

The editor of the university literary journal that published this piece never doubted that it was an actual album, and published the essay in the magazine as an ordinary piece of music criticism. The editor's younger brother, a friend of mine, sold him on me, telling him I wrote some good stuff and they should use my work. (This magazine folded after four issues. My piece was in issue number 3.)

A precious recording tape that Charlie Parker left behind was discovered by accident in the vaults of a record company and just recently saw the light of day—that was the premise I cooked up for the article. Maybe I shouldn't say this myself, but I think this made-up story was plausible: the details were strong, and the writing had real punch. So much so that in the end I nearly came to believe that record existed.

There was considerable reaction to my article when the magazine published it. This was a low-key little college literary journal, generally ignored by readers. But there seemed to be quite a few fans who still idolized Charlie Parker, and the editor received a couple of letters complaining about my **moronic joke** and **thoughtless sacrilege**. Do other people lack a sense of humor? Or is my sense of humor kind of twisted? Hard to say. Some people apparently took the article at face value and even went to music stores in search of the record.

The editor did kick up a bit of a fuss about my having tricked him. I didn't actually fool him, but merely omitted a detailed explanation. Inwardly he must have been pleased that the article drew such a reaction, though most of it was negative. Proof of his enthusiasm came when he told me he'd like to see whatever else I wrote, criticism or original work. (The magazine disappeared before I could show him another piece.)

My article went on as follows:

. . . Who would have ever imagined an unusual lineup like this—Charlie Parker and Antonio Carlos Jobim joining forces? Jimmy Raney on guitar, Jobim on piano, Jimmy Garrison on bass, Roy Haynes on drums—a dream rhythm section so amazing that it makes your heart pound just hearing the names.

And on alto sax—who else but Charlie "Bird" Parker.

Here are the names of the tracks:

SIDE A

(1) Corcovado
(2) Once I Loved (O Amor em Paz)
(3) Just Friends
(4) Bye Bye Blues (Chega de Saudade)

SIDE B

(1) Out of Nowhere
(2) How Insensitive (Insensatez)
(3) Once Again (Outra Vez)
(4) Dindi

With the exception of "Just Friends" and "Out of Nowhere," these are all well-known pieces composed by Carlos Jobim. The two pieces not by Jobim are both standards familiar from Parker's earlier magnificent performances, though of course here they are done in a bossa nova rhythm, a totally new style. (And on these two pieces only, the pianist wasn't Jobim but the versatile veteran pianist Hank Jones.)

So, lover of jazz that you are, what's your first reaction when you hear the title **Charlie Parker Play Bossa Nova**? A yelp of surprise, I would imagine, followed by feelings of curiosity and anticipation. But soon wariness must raise its head—like ominous dark clouds appearing on what had been a beautiful, sunny hillside.

Hold on just a minute—are you telling me that Bird—**Charlie Parker**—is actually playing **bossa nova**? Seriously? Did Bird himself really want to play that kind of music? Or did he give in to commercialism, talked into it by the record company, and reach out for what was **popular** at the time? Even if, say, he genuinely wanted to perform that kind of music, would the style of this 100 percent bebop alto sax player ever harmonize with the cool sounds of Latin American bossa nova?

Setting aside all that—after an eight-year hiatus, was he still master of his instrument? Did he still retain his powerful performing skills and creativity?

Truth be told, I couldn't help feeling uneasy about all that myself. I was dying to hear that music, but at the same time I felt afraid, frightened of disappointment from what I might hear. But now, after I've listened intently to the disc over and over, I can state one thing for sure: I'd even climb up to the roof of a tall building and shout it out so the whole town could hear. If you love jazz, or have any love for music at all, then you absolutely **must** listen to this charming record, the fruit of a passionate heart, and a cool mind . . .

What's surprising, first of all, is the indescribable interplay between Carlos Jobim's simple, economical piano style and Bird's eloquent, uninhibited phrasing. I know you might object that Jobim's voice (he doesn't sing here, so I'm referring only to his instrumental voice) and Bird's voice are so totally different in quality, with dissimilar objectives. We're talking about two very different voices here, so different it might be hard to find any points they share. On top of that, neither one seems to be making much of an effort to revamp their music to fit that of the other. But it's exactly that—the sense of being out of joint, the divergence between the two men's voices—that is the very driving force that gave rise to this uniquely lovely music.

I'd like you to start by listening to the first track on the A side, "Corcovado." Bird doesn't play the opening theme. In fact, he doesn't take up the theme until one phrase at the end. The piece starts with Carlos Jobim quietly playing that familiar theme alone on the piano. The rhythm section is simply mute. The melody calls to mind a young girl seated at a window, gazing out at the beautiful night sky. Most of it is done with single notes, with the occasional no-frills chords added. As if gently tucking a soft cushion under the girl's shoulders.

And once that performance of the piano theme is over, Bird's alto sax quietly enters, a faint twilight shadow slipping through a gap in the curtain.

He's there, before you even realize it. These graceful, seamless phrases are like lovely memories, their names hidden, slipping into your dreams. Like fine wind patterns you never want to disappear, leaving gentle traces on the sand dunes of your heart . . .

I'll omit the rest of the article, which is simply a further description with all the suitable embellishments. The above gives you an idea of the kind of music I'm talking about. Of course it's music that doesn't actually exist. Or, at least, music that **couldn't** possibly exist.

I'LL WRAP UP that story here, and talk about something that took place years later.

For a long time I totally forgot that I'd written that article back in college. My life after school turned out to be more harried and busy than I'd ever imagined, and that review of a make-believe album was nothing more than a lighthearted, irresponsible joke I'd played when I was young. But now, close to fifteen years later, this article unexpectedly reemerged into my life, like a boomerang you threw that whirls back to you when you least expect it.

I was in New York on business and, with time on my hands, took a walk near my hotel and ducked inside a small used-record store I came across on East Fourteenth Street. And in the section of Charlie Parker records I found, of all things, a record titled **Charlie Parker Plays Bossa Nova**. It looked like a bootleg, a privately pressed recording. On the front was a white jacket with no drawing or photo, just the title in sullen black letters. On the back was a list of the tracks and the musicians. Surprisingly, the list of songs and musicians was exactly as I'd made them up back in college. Likewise, Hank Jones sat in for Carlos Jobim on two tracks.

I stood there—still, speechless—record in hand. It felt like some small internal part of me had gone numb. I looked around again. Was this **really** New York? This was downtown New York—no doubt about it. And I was actually here, in a small used-record store. I hadn't wandered into some fantasy world. Nor was I having some super-realistic dream.

I slipped the record out of its jacket. It had a white label, with the title and names of the songs. No sign of a record company logo. I examined the vinyl itself and found four distinct tracks on each side. I went over and asked the long-haired young guy at the register if

I could take a listen to the album. No, he replied. The store turntable's broken. Sorry about that.

The price on the record was $35. I wavered for a long time about whether to buy it. In the end, I left the shop empty-handed. I figured, it's got to be somebody's idea of a silly joke. Somebody, on a whim, had faked a record based on my long-ago description of an imaginary recording. Took a different record that had four tracks on each side, soaked it in water, peeled off the label, and glued on a homemade one. Any way you look at it, it was ridiculous to pay $35 for a bogus record like that.

I went to a Spanish restaurant near the hotel and had some beer and a simple dinner by myself. Afterward, as I was strolling around aimlessly, a wave of regret suddenly welled up in me. I should have bought that record. Even if it was a fake, and even if it was way overpriced, I should have bought it, at the very least as a souvenir of all the twists and turns my life had taken. I went straight back to Fourteenth Street. I hurried, but the record store was closed by the time I got there. On the shutter was a sign that said the store opened at 11:30 a.m. and closed at 7:30 p.m. on weekdays.

The next morning, just before noon, I went over to the store again. A middle-aged guy—thinning hair, in a disheveled, round-necked sweater—was sipping coffee and reading the sports section of the paper. The coffee seemed freshly brewed, for a pleasant smell wafted faintly through the store. The store had just opened, and I was the only customer. An old tune by Pharoah Sanders filtered through the small speaker on the ceiling. I assumed the man was the store's owner. I thumbed through the Charlie Parker section, but that record was nowhere to be found. I was sure I'd returned the record to that section yesterday. Thinking it might have gotten mixed in elsewhere, I rifled through every bin in the jazz section. But as hard as I looked, no luck. Had someone else bought it since my visit yesterday? I went over to the register and spoke to the middle-aged guy. "I'm looking for a jazz record I saw here yesterday."

"Which record?" he asked, eyes never wavering from **The New York Times**.

"**Charlie Parker Plays Bossa Nova**," I said.

He laid down his paper, took off his thin, metal-framed reading glasses, and slowly turned to face me. "I'm sorry. Could you repeat that?"

I did. The man said nothing, and took another sip of coffee. He shook his head slightly. "There's no such record."

"Of course," I said.

"If you'd like **Perry Como Sings Jimi Hendrix**, we have that in stock."

"**Perry Como Sings—**" I got that far before I realized he was joking, even though he did so with a straight face. "But I really **did** see it," I insisted. "I was sure it was produced as a joke, I mean."

"You saw that record **here?**"

"Yesterday afternoon. Right here." I described the record, the jacket and songs on it. How it had been priced at $35.

"There's gotta be some mistake. We've never had that kind of record. I do all the purchasing and pricing of jazz records myself, and if a record like that had crossed my desk, I would definitely have remembered it. Whether I wanted to or not."

He shook his head and put his reading glasses back on. He went back to reading the sports section, but then, as if he'd had second thoughts, he removed his glasses, smiled, and gazed steadily at me. "But if you ever do get hold of that record," he said, "let me listen to it, okay?"

THERE'S ONE MORE THING that came later on.

This happened a long time after that incident (in fact, quite recently). One night I had a dream about Charlie Parker. In the dream, he performed "Corcovado" just for me—**for me alone**. Solo alto sax, no rhythm section.

Sunlight was shining in from some gap somewhere, and Parker was standing by himself in a spot lit up by the long, vertical beam. Morning light, I assumed.

Fresh, honest light that was still free of any superfluous meaning. Bird's face, facing me, was hidden in deep shadow, but I could somehow make out the dark double-breasted suit, white shirt, and brightly colored tie. And the alto sax he had, which was absurdly filthy, covered in dirt and rust. There was one bent key he'd barely kept in place by taping the handle of a spoon to it. When I saw that, I was puzzled. Even Bird wouldn't be able to get a decent sound out of that poor excuse for an instrument.

Suddenly, right then, my nose detected an amazingly fragrant aroma of coffee. What an entrancing smell. The aroma of hot, strong black coffee. My nostrils twitched with pleasure. For all the temptations of that smell, I never took my eyes off Bird. If I did, even for a second, he might vanish from sight.

I'm not sure why, but I knew then it

was a dream. That I was seeing Bird in a dream. That happens sometimes. When I'm dreaming I know for certain—**This is a dream**. And I was strangely impressed that in the midst of a dream I could catch, so very clearly, the enticing smell of coffee.

Bird finally put lips to the mouthpiece and carefully blew one subdued sound, as if checking the condition of the reed. And once that sound had faded away over time, he quietly lined up a few more notes the same way. The notes floated there for a time, then gently fell to the ground. They fell to the ground, one and all, and once they were swallowed up by the silence, Bird sent out a series of deeper, more resilient notes into the air. That's how "Corcovado" started.

How to describe that music? Looking back on it, this music Bird played just for me in my dream felt less like a stream of sound than like a momentary, total irradiation. I can vividly remember the music being there. But I can't reproduce it. With time, it's faded away, like the inability to describe the design of a mandala. What I can say is that it was music that reached to the deep recesses of my soul, all the way down to the very core. I was certain that kind of music existed in the world—music that made you feel like something in the very structure of your body had been reconfigured, ever so slightly, now that you'd experienced it.

"I WAS ONLY THIRTY-FOUR when I died," Bird said to me. "Thirty-four!" At least I think he was saying it to me. Since we were the only two people in the room.

I didn't know how to respond. It's hard in dreams to do the right thing. So I stayed silent, waiting for him to go on.

"Think about it—what it is to die at thirty-four," Bird went on.

I thought about how I'd feel if I'd died at thirty-four. When I'd only just begun so many things in life.

"That's right. I'd only begun things myself," Bird said. "Only begun to live my life. But then I looked around me and it was all over." He silently shook his head. His entire face was still hidden in shadow, so I couldn't see his expression. His dirty, battered saxophone hung from the strap around his neck.

"Death always comes on suddenly," Bird said. "But it also takes its time. Like the beautiful phrases that come into your head. It lasts an instant, yet those instants can draw out forever. As long as from the East Coast to the West Coast—or to infinity, even. The concept of time is lost there. In that sense, I might have been dead even as I lived out my life. But actual death is a crushing. What's existed until then suddenly and completely vanishes. Returns to nothingness. In my case, that existence was **me**."

He looked down for a time, staring at his instrument. And then he spoke again.

"Do you know what I was thinking about when I died?" Bird asked. "My mind had just one thought—a single melody. I kept on humming that melody over and over in my head. It just wouldn't let go. That happens, right? A tune gets stuck in your head. That melody was a phrase from the third movement of Beethoven's Piano Concerto no. 1. This melody."

Bird softly hummed the melody. I recognized it. The solo piano part.

"This is the one Beethoven melody that really swings," Bird said. "I've always liked his Concerto no. 1. I've listened to it I don't know how many times. The SP record with Schnabel on piano. But it's strange, don't you think? That me—Charlie Parker—when I died I was humming, of all things, a Beethoven melody in my mind, over and over. And then came darkness. Like a curtain falling." Bird gave a little laugh, his voice hoarse.

No words came to me. What could I possibly say about the death of Charlie Parker?

"Anyway, I need to thank you," Bird said. "You gave me life again, this one time. And had me play bossa nova. Nothing could make me happier. Of course being alive and actually playing would have been even more exciting. But even after dying, this was a truly wonderful experience. Since I always loved new music."

So did you appear here today in order to thank me?

"That's right," Bird said, as if reading my mind. "I stopped by to express my thanks. To say thank you. I hope you enjoyed my music."

I nodded. I should have said something, but couldn't for the life of me come up with the right response.

"**Perry Como Sings Jimi Hendrix,** eh?" Bird murmured, as if recalling. And chuckled again in a hoarse voice.

And then he vanished. First his saxophone disappeared, next the light shining in from somewhere. And finally, Bird himself was gone.

WHEN I WOKE UP from the dream, the clock next to my bed read 3:30 a.m. It was still dark out, of course. The fragrance of coffee that should have filled the room was gone. There was no fragrance at all. I went to the kitchen and gulped down a couple of glasses of water. I sat down at the dining table, and tried once more to reproduce, if even a little, that amazing music that Bird had played just for me. I couldn't recall a single phrase. But I could remember what Bird had said. Before they faded from memory, I wrote down his words, with a ballpoint pen in a notebook, as accurately as I could. That was the only action I could take. Bird had visited my dream in order to thank me— that much, I recalled. To thank me for allowing him the opportunity, so many years ago, to play bossa nova. And he grabbed an instrument that happened to be around and played "Corcovado" just for me.

Can you believe it?

You'd better. Because it happened.

It really did.

WITH THE BEATLES

WHAT I FIND STRANGE about growing old isn't that I've gotten older. Not that the youthful me from the past has, without my realizing it, aged. What catches me off guard is, rather, how people from the same generation as me have become elderly, how all the pretty, vivacious girls I used to know are now old enough to have a couple of grandkids. It's a little disconcerting—sad, even. Though I never feel sad at the fact that I have similarly aged.

I think what makes me feel sad

about the girls I knew growing old is that it forces me to admit, all over again, that my youthful dreams are gone forever. The death of a dream can be, in a way, sadder than that of a living being. Sometimes it all seems so unfair.

There's one girl—a woman who used to be a girl, I mean—whom I remember well. I don't know her name, though. And, naturally, I don't know where she is now or what she's doing. What I do know about her is that she went to the same high school as I did, and was in the same year (since the badge on her shirt was the same color as mine), and that she really liked the Beatles. Other than that, I know nothing about her.

This was in 1964, at the height of Beatlemania. It was early autumn. The new school semester had begun and things were starting to fall into a routine again. She was hurrying down the long, dim hallway of the old school building, her skirt fluttering. I was the only other person there. She was clutching an LP to her chest as if it were something precious. The LP **With the Beatles**. The one with the striking black-and-white photograph of the four Beatles in half shadow. For some reason, I'm not sure why, I have a clear memory that it was the original, British version of the album, not the American or the Japanese version.

She was a beautiful girl. At least, to me then, she looked gorgeous. She wasn't tall, but she had long black hair, slim legs, and a lovely fragrance. (That could be a false memory, I don't know. Maybe she didn't give off any scent at all. But that's what I remember, as if, when she passed, an enchanting, alluring fragrance wafted in my direction.) She had me under her spell—that beautiful, nameless girl clutching **With the Beatles** to her chest.

My heart started to pound, I gasped for breath, and it was as if all sound had ceased, as if I'd sunk to the bottom of a pool. All I could hear was a bell ringing faintly, deep in my ears. As if someone were desperately trying to send me a vital message. All this took only ten or fifteen seconds. It was over before I knew it, and the critical message contained there, like the core of all dreams, disappeared. Just like most important things do that happen in life.

A dimly lit hallway in a high school, a beautiful girl, the hem of her skirt swirling, **With the Beatles**.

That was the only time I saw that girl. In the two years between then and my graduation, we never once crossed paths again. Which is pretty strange if you think about it. The high school I attended was a fairly large public school at the top of a hill in Kobe, with about 650 students in each grade. (We were the so-called Baby Boomer generation, so there were a lot of us.) Not everyone knew one another. In fact, I didn't know the names or recognize the vast majority of the kids in the school. But, still, since I went to school almost every day, and often used that hallway, it struck me as almost outrageous that I never once saw that beautiful girl again. I looked for her every time I used that hallway.

Had she vanished, like smoke? Or, on that early-autumn afternoon, had I seen not a real person but a vision of some kind? Perhaps I had idealized her in my mind at the instant that we passed each other, to the point where even if I actually saw her again I wouldn't recognize her? (I think the last possibility is the most likely.)

Later, I got to know a few women, and

went out with them. And every time I met a new woman it felt as though I were unconsciously longing to relive that dazzling moment I'd experienced in a dim school hallway back in the fall of 1964. That silent, insistent thrill in my heart, the breathless feeling in my chest, the bell ringing gently in my ears.

Sometimes I was able to recapture this feeling, at other times not. (Unfortunately, the bell didn't ring enough.) And other times I managed to grab hold of it, only to let it slip through my fingers. In any event, the emotions that surged when this happened came to serve as a kind of gauge I used to measure the intensity of my yearning.

When I couldn't get that sensation in the real world, I would quietly let my memory of those feelings awaken inside me. In this way, memory became one of my most valued emotional tools, a means of survival, even. Like a warm kitten, softly curled inside an oversized coat pocket, fast asleep.

On to the Beatles.

A year before I saw that girl was when the Beatles first became wildly popular. By April of 1964, they'd captured the top five spots on the American singles charts. Pop music had never seen anything like Beatlemania. These were the five hit songs: (1) "Can't Buy Me Love"; (2) "Twist and Shout"; (3) "She Loves You"; (4) "I Want to Hold Your Hand"; (5) "Please Please Me." The single "Can't Buy Me Love" alone had more than two million preorders, making it double platinum before the actual record went on sale.

The Beatles were, of course, also hugely popular in Japan. Turn on the radio and chances were you'd hear one of their songs. I liked their songs myself and knew all their hits. Ask me to sing them, and I could. At home when I was studying (or pretending to study), most of the time I had the radio blasting away. But, truth be told, I was never a fervent Beatles fan. I never actively sought out their songs. For me, it was passive listening, pop music flowing out of the tiny speakers of my Panasonic transistor radio, in one ear and out the other, barely registering. Background music for my adolescence. Musical wallpaper.

In high school and in college, I didn't buy a single Beatles record. I was much more into jazz and classical music, and that was what I listened to when I wanted to focus on music. I saved up to buy jazz records, requested tunes by Miles Davis and Thelonious Monk at jazz bars, and went to classical music concerts. It was only much later that I bought my first Beatles record and seriously listened to their music. But that's a story for another time.

THIS MIGHT SEEM STRANGE, but it wasn't until I was in my mid-thirties that I sat down and listened to **With the Beatles** from beginning to end. Despite the fact that the image of the girl carrying that LP in the hallway of our high school had never left me, for the longest time I didn't feel like actually giving it a listen. I wasn't particularly interested in knowing what sort of music was etched into the grooves of the vinyl disk she had clutched so tightly.

When I was in my mid-thirties, well past childhood and adolescence, my first impression of the album was that it wasn't that great, or at least not the kind of music to take your breath away. Of the fourteen tracks on the album, six were covers of other artists' works. The covers of the Marvelettes' "Please Mr. Postman" and Chuck Berry's "Roll Over Beethoven" were well done, and impress me even when I listen to them now, but, still, they were cover versions. And of the eight original songs, apart from Paul's "All My Loving," none were amazing. There were no hit singles, and while I applaud their enterprising spirit in putting out albums that included only new material and no recycled singles, to my ears the Beatles' first album, **Please Please Me**, recorded basically in one take, was more vibrant and compelling. Even so, likely thanks to Beatles fans' unquenchable desire for new songs, this second album debuted in the number one spot in the U.K., a position it held for twenty-one weeks. (In the U.S., the title of the album was changed to **Meet the Beatles**, and included some different tracks, though the cover design stayed almost the same.) What probably accounted for this phenomenal success was their fans' passionate desire—like travelers' thirst for water after traversing a desert—for a fresh supply of Beatles music, plus the memorable monochrome cover photo, in half shadow, of the four of them.

WHAT PULLED ME IN was the vision of that girl clutching the album as if it were something priceless. Take away the photograph on the album cover and the scene might not have bewitched me as it did. There was the music, for sure. But there was something else, something far bigger. And, in an instant, that tableau was etched in my heart—a kind of spiritual landscape that could be found **only** there, at a set age, in a set place, and at a set moment in time.

For me, the major event of the following year, 1965, wasn't President Johnson ordering the bombing of North Vietnam and the escalation of the war, or the discovery of a new species of wildcat on the island of Iriomote, but the fact that I acquired a girlfriend. She had been in the same class as me in freshman year, but it wasn't until sophomore year that we started going out.

To avoid any misunderstanding, I'd like to preface this by saying that I'm not good-looking and was never a star athlete, and my grades in school were less than stellar. My singing left something to be desired, too, and I didn't have a way with words. When I was in school, and in the years after that, I never once had girls flocking around me. That's one of the few things I can say with certainty in this uncertain life. Still, there always seemed to be a girl around who was, for whatever reason, attracted to me. I have no clue why, but I was able to enjoy some pleasant, intimate times with those girls. I got to be good friends with some of them, and occasionally took it to the next level. The girl I'm talking about here was one of these—the first girl I had a really **close** relationship with.

This first girlfriend of mine was petite and charming. That summer, I went on dates with her once a week. One afternoon I kissed her small yet full lips and touched her breasts through her bra. She was wearing a sleeveless white dress and her hair had a citrusy shampoo scent.

She had almost no interest in the Beatles. She wasn't into jazz, either. What she liked to listen to was more mellow music, what you might call middle-class music—the Mantovani Orchestra, Percy Faith, Roger Williams, Andy Williams, Nat King Cole, and the like. (At the time, **middle class** wasn't a derogatory term at all.) There were piles of such records at her house—what nowadays is classified as easy listening.

That afternoon, she put a record on the turntable in her living room—her family had a large, impressive stereo system—and we sat on the big, comfy sofa and kissed. Her family had gone out somewhere, and it was just the two of us. Truthfully, in a situation like that I didn't really care what sort of music was playing.

What I remember about the summer of 1965 was her white dress, the citrusy scent of her shampoo, the formidable feel of her wire bra (a bra back then was more like a fortress than like an item of underwear), and the elegant performance of Max Steiner's "Theme from **A Summer**

Place" by the Percy Faith Orchestra. Even now, whenever I hear "Theme from **A Summer Place**," that large, comfy sofa comes to mind.

Incidentally, several years later—1968, as I recall, around the same time that Robert Kennedy was assassinated—the man who had been our homeroom teacher when we were in the same class hanged himself from the lintel in his house. He'd taught social studies. An ideological impasse was said to be the cause of his suicide.

An ideological impasse?

But it's true—in the late sixties people sometimes took their own lives because they'd hit a wall, ideologically. Though not all that often.

I get a really strange feeling when I think that on that afternoon, as my girlfriend and I were clumsily making out on the sofa, with Percy Faith's pretty music in the background, that social studies teacher was, step by step, heading toward his fatal ideological dead end, or, to put it another way, toward that silent, tight knot in the rope. I even feel bad about it sometimes. Among all the teachers I knew, he was one of the best. Whether he was successful or not is another question, but he always tried to treat his students fairly. I never spoke to him outside of class, but that was how I remembered him.

Like 1964, 1965 was the year of the Beatles. They released "Eight Days a Week" in February, "Ticket to Ride" in April, "Help!" in July, and "Yesterday" in September—all of which topped the U.S. charts. It seemed as if we were hearing their music almost all the time. It was everywhere, surrounding us, like wallpaper meticulously applied to every single inch of the walls.

When the Beatles' music wasn't playing, it was the Rolling Stones' "(I Can't Get No) Satisfaction," or the Byrds' "Mr. Tambourine Man," or "My Girl" by the Temptations, or the Righteous Brothers' "You've Lost That Lovin' Feelin'," or the Beach Boys' "Help Me, Rhonda." Diana Ross and the Supremes also had one hit after another. A constant soundtrack of this kind of wonderful, joyful music filtered out through my little Panasonic transistor radio. It was truly an astounding year for pop music, one that took your breath away.

I've heard it said that the happiest time in our lives is the period when pop songs really mean something to us, really get to us. It may be true. Or maybe not. Pop songs may, after all, be nothing but pop songs. And perhaps our lives are merely decorative, expendable items, a burst of fleeting color and nothing more.

My girlfriend's house was near the Kobe radio station that I always tuned in to. I think her father imported, or perhaps exported, medical equipment. I don't know the details. At any rate, he owned his own company, which seemed to be doing well. Their home was in a pine grove near the sea. I heard that it used to be the summer villa of some business-man and that her family had bought and remodeled it. The pine trees rustled in the sea breeze. It was the perfect place to listen to "Theme from **A Summer Place**."

YEARS LATER, I happened to see a late-night TV broadcast of the 1959 movie **A Summer Place**. It starred Troy Donahue and Sandra Dee, and was a typical Hollywood film about young love, but nevertheless it held together well. Percy Faith had a hit with a cover version of the

Max Steiner theme song of the same title. In the movie, there is a pine grove by the sea, which sways in the summer breeze in time to the horn section. That scene of the pine trees swaying in the wind struck me as a metaphor for the young people's raging sexual desire. But that may just have been my take on it, my own biased view.

In the movie, Troy Donahue and Sandra Dee are swept up in that kind of overpowering sexual wind and, because of it, encounter all kinds of real-world problems. Misunderstandings are followed by reconciliations, obstacles are cleared up like fog lifting, and in the end the two come together and are married. In Hollywood in the fifties, a happy ending always involved marriage—the creation of an environment in which lovers could have sex legally. My girlfriend and I, of course, didn't get married. We were still in high school, and all we did was clumsily grope and make out on the sofa with "Theme from **A Summer Place**" playing in the background.

"You know something?" she said to me on the sofa, in a small voice, as if she were making a confession. "I'm the really jealous type."

"Seriously?" I said.

"I wanted to make sure you knew that."

"Okay."

"Sometimes it hurts a lot to be so jealous."

I silently stroked her hair. It was beyond me at the time to imagine how burning jealousy felt, what caused it, what it led to. I was too preoccupied with my own emotions.

As a side note, Troy Donahue, that handsome young star, later got caught up in alcohol and drugs, stopped making movies, and was even homeless for a time. Sandra Dee, too, struggled with alcoholism. Donahue married the popular actress Suzanne Pleshette in 1964, but they divorced eight months later. Dee married the singer Bobby Darin in 1960, but they divorced in 1967. This is obviously totally unrelated to the plot of **A Summer Place**. And unrelated to my and my girlfriend's fate.

My girlfriend had an older brother and a younger sister. The younger sister was in her second year of junior high but was a good two inches taller than her older sister. She wasn't particularly cute. Plus, she wore thick glasses. But my girlfriend was very fond of her kid sister. "Her grades in school are really good," she told me. I think my girlfriend's grades, by the way, were only fair to middling. Like my own, most likely.

One time, we let her younger sister tag along with us to the movies. There was some reason that we had to. The film was **The Sound of Music**. The theater was packed, so we had to sit near the front, and I remember that watching that 70 mm wide-screen film so close up made my eyes ache by the end. My girlfriend, though, was crazy about the songs in the film. She bought the soundtrack LP and listened to it endlessly. Me, I was much more into John Coltrane's magical version of "My Favorite Things," but I figured that bringing that up with her was pointless, so I never did.

Her younger sister didn't seem to like me much. Whenever we saw each other she looked at me with strange eyes, totally devoid of emotion—as if she were judging whether some dried fish at the back of the fridge was still edible or not. And, for some reason, that look always left me feeling guilty. When she looked at me, it was as though she were ignoring the outside (granted, it wasn't much to look at anyway) and could see right through me, down to the depths of my being. I may have felt that way because I really did have shame and guilt in my heart.

My girlfriend's brother was four years older than she was, so he would have been at least twenty then. She didn't introduce him to me and hardly ever mentioned him. If he happened to come up in conversation, she deftly changed the subject. I can see now that her attitude was a bit unnatural. Not that I thought much about it. I wasn't that interested in her family. What drew me to her was something very different, a much more urgent impulse.

The first time I met her brother and spoke with him was toward the end of autumn in 1965.

That Sunday, I went to my girlfriend's house to pick her up. We went on dates pretending we were going to the library to study, so I always put various study-related items in my shoulder bag to keep up the facade. Like a novice criminal making up a flimsy alibi.

I rang the bell over and over, but no one answered. I paused for a while, then rang it again, repeatedly, until I finally heard someone moving slowly toward the door. It was my girlfriend's older brother.

He was a shade taller than me and a bit on the hefty side. Not flabby, but more like an athlete who, for some reason, can't exercise for a while and packs on a few extra pounds, just temporary fat. He had broad shoulders but a relatively long, thin neck. His hair was disheveled, sticking out all over the place, as if he'd just woken up. It looked stiff and coarse, and he seemed about two weeks overdue for a haircut. He had on a crew-neck navy-blue sweater, the neck loose, and gray sweats that were baggy around the knees. His look was the complete opposite of my girlfriend's—she was always neat and clean and well groomed.

He squinted at me for a while, like some scruffy animal that had, after a long hibernation, crawled out into the sunlight.

"I'm guessing you are . . . Sayoko's friend?" He said this before I got a word out. He cleared his throat. His voice was sleepy, but I could sense a spark of interest in it.

"That's right," I said, and introduced myself. "I was supposed to come here at eleven."

"Sayoko's not here right now," he said.

"Not here," I said, repeating his words.

"She's out somewhere. She's not at home."

"But I was supposed to come and pick her up today at eleven."

"Is that right?" her brother said. He glanced up at the wall beside him, as if checking a clock. But there was no clock there, just a white plaster wall. He reluctantly turned his gaze back to me. "That may be, but the fact is she's not at home."

I had no clue what I should do. And neither did her brother, apparently. He gave a leisurely yawn and scratched the back of his head. All his actions were slow and measured.

"Doesn't seem like anybody's at home now," he said. "When I got up a while ago nobody was here. They must have all gone out, but I don't know where."

I didn't say anything.

"My father's probably out golfing. My sisters must have gone out to have some fun. But my mom being out, too, is a little odd. That doesn't happen often."

I refrained from speculating. This wasn't my family.

"But if Sayoko promised she'd be here, I'm sure she'll be back soon," her brother said. "Why don't you come inside and wait?"

"I don't want to bother you. I'll just hang out somewhere for a while and then come back," I said.

"Nah, it's no bother," he said firmly. "Much more of a bother to have you ring the bell again and me have to come and open the front door. So come on in."

I had no other choice, so I went inside, and he led me to the living room. The living room with the sofa on which she and I had made out in the summer. I sat down on it, and my girlfriend's brother eased himself into an armchair facing me. And once again let out a long yawn.

"You're Sayoko's friend, right?" he asked again, as if making doubly sure.

"That's right," I said, giving the same reply.

"Not Yuko's friend?"

I shook my head. Yuko was her taller kid sister.

"Is it interesting going out with Sayoko?" her brother asked, a look of curiosity in his eyes.

I had no clue how to respond, so I stayed silent. He sat there, waiting for my reply.

"It's fun, yes," I said, finally finding what I hoped were the right words.

"It's fun, but it's not interesting?"

"No, that's not what I mean . . ." My words petered out.

"No matter," her brother said. "Interesting or fun—no difference between the two, I suppose. Hey, have you had breakfast?"

"I have, yes."

"I'm going to make some toast. Sure you don't want any?"

"No, I'm fine," I replied.

"You sure?"

"I'm sure."

"How about coffee?"

"I'm fine."

I could have done with some coffee, but I hesitated to get more involved with my girlfriend's family, especially when she wasn't at home.

He stood up without a word and left the room. Probably went to the kitchen to make breakfast. After a while, I heard the clatter of dishes and cups. I stayed there alone on the sofa, politely sitting up straight, my hands in my lap, waiting for her to come back from wherever she was. The clock now read 11:15.

I scanned my memory to see if we really had decided that I would come at eleven. But, no matter how much I thought it over, I was sure that I'd gotten the date and time correct. We'd talked on the phone the night before and had confirmed it then. She wasn't the type to forget or blow off a promise. And it was odd, indeed, for her and her family to all go off on a Sunday morning and leave her older brother by himself.

Puzzled by it all, I sat there patiently. Time passed excruciatingly slowly. I'd hear the occasional sound from the kitchen—the faucet turning on, the clatter of a spoon mixing something, the sound of a cupboard opening and closing. This brother seemed the type who had to make a racket, whatever he did. But that was it, as far as sounds went. No wind blowing outside, no dogs barking. Like invisible mud, the silence steadily crept into my ears and plugged them up. I had to gulp a few times to unblock them.

Some music would have been nice. "Theme from **A Summer Place**,"

"Edelweiss," "Moon River"—anything. I wasn't picky. Just some music. But I couldn't very well turn on the stereo in somebody else's house without permission. I looked around for something to read but didn't spot any newspapers or magazines. I checked out what was inside my shoulder bag. I almost always had a paperback I was reading in my bag, but not that day. As luck would have it, that was the day I'd forgotten to bring a book.

The only book I had in my bag that day was a supplementary reader for our school textbook, **Japanese Language and Literature**. I reluctantly pulled it out and started flipping through the pages. I wasn't what you'd call a **reader**, who goes through books systematically and attentively, but more the type who finds it hard to pass the time without something to read. I could never just sit, still and silent. I always had to be turning the pages of a book or listening to music, one or the other. When there was no book lying around, I'd grab anything printed. I'd read a phone book, an instruction manual for a steam iron. Compared with those kinds of reading material, a supplementary reader for a Japanese-language textbook was far better.

I randomly flipped through the fiction and essays in the book. A few pieces were by foreign authors, but most were by well-known modern Japanese writers—Ryūnosuke Akutagawa, Junichirō Tanizaki, Kobo Abe, and the like. And appended to each work—all excerpts, except for a handful of very short stories—were some questions. Most of these questions were totally meaningless. With meaningless questions, it's hard (or impossible) to determine logically if an answer is correct or not. I doubted whether even the authors of the selections themselves would have been able to decide. Things like "What can you glean from this passage about the writer's stance toward war?" or "When the author describes the waxing and waning of the moon, what sort of symbolic effect is created?" You could give almost any answer. If you said that the description of the waxing and waning of the moon was simply a description of the waxing and waning of the moon, and created no symbolic effect, no one could say with certainty that your answer was wrong. Of course there was a relatively reasonable answer, but I didn't really think that arriving at a relatively reasonable answer was one of the goals of studying literature.

Be that as it may, I killed time by trying to conjure up answers to each of these questions. And, in most cases, what sprang to mind—in my brain, which was still growing and developing, struggling every day to attain a kind of psychological independence—were the sorts of answers that were relatively unreasonable but not necessarily wrong. Maybe that tendency was one of the reasons that my grades at school were no great shakes.

While this was going on, my girlfriend's brother came back to the living room. His hair was still sticking out in all directions, but, maybe because he'd had breakfast, his eyes weren't as sleepy as before. He held a large white mug, which had a picture of a First World War German biplane, with two machine guns in front of the cockpit, printed on the side. This had to be his own special mug. I couldn't picture my girlfriend drinking from a mug like that.

"You really don't want any coffee?" he asked.

I shook my head. "No. I'm fine. Really."

His sweater was festooned with bread crumbs. The knees of his sweats, too. He had probably been starving and had gobbled down the toast without caring about crumbs going everywhere. I could imagine that bugging my girlfriend, since she always looked so neat and tidy. I liked to be neat and tidy myself, a shared quality that was part of why we got along, I think.

Her brother glanced up at the wall. There was a clock on this wall. The hands of the clock showed nearly 11:30.

"SHE ISN'T BACK YET, is she? Where the heck could she have gone off to?"

I said nothing in response.

"What're you reading?"

"A supplementary reader for our Japanese textbook."

"Hmm," he said, frowning slightly. "Is it interesting?"

"Not particularly. I just don't have anything else to read."

"Could you show it to me?"

I passed him the book over the low table. Coffee cup in his left hand, he took the book with his right. I was worried that he'd spill coffee on it. That seemed about to happen. But he didn't spill. He put his cup down on the glass tabletop with a clink, and he held the book in both hands and starting flipping through.

"So what part were you reading?"

"Just now I was reading Akutagawa's story 'Spinning Gears.' There's only part of the story there, not the whole thing."

He gave this some thought. "'Spinning Gears' is one I've never read. Though I did read his story 'Kappa' a long time ago. Isn't 'Spinning Gears' a pretty dark story?"

"It is. Since he wrote it right before he died."

"Akutagawa committed suicide, didn't he?"

"That's right," I said. Akutagawa overdosed when he was thirty-five. My supplementary reader's notes said that "Spinning Gears" was published posthumously, in 1927. The story was almost a last will and testament.

"Hmm," my girlfriend's brother said. "D'ya think you could read it for me?"

I looked at him in surprise. "Read it aloud, you mean?"

"Yeah. I've always liked to have people read to me. I'm not such a great reader myself."

"I'm not good at reading aloud."

"I don't mind. You don't have to be

good. Just read it in the right order, and that'll be fine. I mean, it doesn't look like we have anything else to do."

"It's a pretty neurotic, depressing story, though," I said.

"Sometimes I like to hear that kind of story. Like, to fight evil with evil."

He handed the book back, picked up the coffee cup with the picture of the biplane and its Iron Crosses, and took a sip. Then he sank back in his armchair and waited for the reading to begin.

That was how I ended up that Sunday reading part of Akutagawa's "Spinning Gears" to my girlfriend's eccentric older brother. I was a bit reluctant at first, but I warmed to the job. The supplementary reader had the two final sections of the story—"Red Lights" and "Airplane"— but I just read "Airplane." It was about eight pages long, and it ended with the line "Won't someone be good enough to strangle me as I sleep?" Akutagawa killed himself right after writing this line.

I finished reading, but still no one in the family had come home. The phone didn't ring, and no crows cawed outside. It was perfectly still all around. The autumn sunlight lit up the living room through the lace curtains. Time alone made its slow, steady way forward. My girlfriend's brother sat there, arms folded, eyes shut, as if savoring the final lines I'd read: "I don't have the strength to go on writing. It is painful beyond words to keep living when I feel like this. Won't someone be good enough to strangle me as I sleep?"

Whether you liked the writing or not, one thing was clear: this wasn't the right story to read on a bright, clear Sunday. I closed the book and glanced up at the clock on the wall. It was just past twelve.

"There must have been some kind of

misunderstanding," I said. "I think I'll be going." I started to get up from the sofa. My mother had drummed it into me from childhood that you shouldn't bother people at home when it was time to have a meal. For better or for worse, this had seeped into my being and become a reflexive habit.

"You've come all this way, so how about waiting another thirty minutes?" my girl-friend's brother asked. "How about you wait another thirty minutes, and if she's not back by then you can leave?"

His words were oddly distinct, and I sat back down and rested my hands in my lap again.

"You're very good at reading aloud," he said, sounding genuinely impressed. "Has anybody ever told you that?"

I shook my head.

"Unless you really grasp the content,

you can't read like you did. The last part was especially good."

"Oh," I answered vaguely. I felt my cheeks redden a bit. The praise seemed misdirected, and it made me uncomfortable. But the sense I was getting was that I was in for another thirty minutes of conversation with him. He seemed to need someone to talk to.

He placed his palms firmly together in front of him, as if praying, then suddenly came out with this: "This might sound like a weird question, but have you ever had your memory stop?"

"Stop?"

"What I'm talking about is, like, from one point in time to the next you can't remember at all where you were, or what you were doing."

I shook my head. "I don't think I've ever had that."

"So you remember the time sequence and details of what you've done?"

"If it's something that happened recently, yes, I'd say so."

"Hmm," he said, and scratched the back of his head for a moment, and then spoke. "I suppose that's normal."

I waited for him to continue.

"Actually, I've had several times where my memory has just slipped away. Like at three p.m. my memory cuts out, and the next thing I know it's seven p.m. And I can't remember where I was, or what I was doing, during those four hours. And it's not like something special happened to me. Like I got hit on the head or got sloppy drunk or anything. I'm just doing my usual thing and without warning my memory cuts out. I can't predict when it's going to happen. And I have no clue for how many hours, how many days, even, my memory will vanish."

"I see," I murmured, to let him know I was following along.

"Imagine you've recorded a Mozart symphony on a tape recorder. And when you play it back the sound jumps from the middle of the second movement to the middle of the third, and what should be in between has just vanished. That's what it's like. When I say 'vanished,' I don't mean that there's a silent section of tape. It's just gone. Like the day after today is two days from now. Do you get what I'm saying?"

"I guess so," I said in an uncertain tone.

"If it's music, it's kind of inconvenient, but no real harm, right? But, if it happens in your real life, then it's a pain, believe me . . . You get what I mean?"

I nodded.

"You go to the dark side of the moon and come back empty-handed."

I nodded again. I wasn't sure I completely grasped the analogy.

"It's caused by a genetic disorder, and clear-cut cases like mine are pretty rare. One person out of tens of thousands will have the disorder. And even then there'll be differences among them, of course. In my last year of junior high, I was examined by a neurologist at the university hospital. My mom took me. The condition has a name, some annoyingly long term. I forgot it a long time ago. Makes me wonder who came up with a name like that."

He paused, then went on: "In other words, it's a condition where the sequence of your memory gets messed up. One part of your memory—like the example I gave of part of a Mozart symphony—gets stashed away in the wrong drawer. And it's next to impossible, or actually impossible, to ever find it again. That's how they explained it to me. It's not the kind of terrible disorder that can be fatal, or where you gradually lose your mind. But it does cause problems in daily life. They told me the name of the disorder and gave me some medication to take, but the pills don't do a thing. They're just a placebo."

For a moment, my girlfriend's brother was silent, studying me closely to see whether I understood. It was as if he were outside a house staring in through a window.

"I have these episodes once or twice a year now," he finally said. "Not so often, but the frequency isn't the issue. When it happens it causes real problems. Even if it's only seldom, it's pretty awful having that kind of memory loss and not knowing **when** it'll happen. You get that, right?"

"Uh-huh," I said vaguely. It was all I could do to follow his odd, rapid-fire story.

"Like, say it happens to me, my memory suddenly cuts out, and during that lapse I take a huge hammer and bash somebody's head in, somebody I don't like. No way you can just write that off by saying, 'Well, now, that's awkward.' Am I right?"

"I'd say so."

"The cops'll get involved and if I tell them, 'The thing is, my memory flew away,' they're not going to buy that, now, are they?"

I shook my head.

"There are actually a couple of people I don't like at all. Guys who really piss me off. My dad's one of them. But when

I'm lucid I'm not about to bash my dad on the head with a hammer, am I? I'm able to control myself. But when my memory cuts out, I have no clue what I'm doing."

I inclined my head a fraction, withholding any opinion.

"The doctor said there's no danger of that happening. It's not like, while my memory's gone, somebody hijacks my personality. Like Dr. Jekyll and Mr. Hyde. I'm always myself. Even when my memory cuts out, I act like I usually do. It's just that the recorded part skips from the middle of the second movement to the middle of the third. So it's impossible that during that interval I take out a hammer and smash somebody's head. I'm always able to control who I am, and act normally for the most part. Mozart doesn't suddenly transform into Stravinsky. Mozart remains Mozart—it's just that one part disappears into a drawer somewhere."

He clammed up at this point and took a sip from his biplane coffee cup. I was wishing I could have some coffee myself.

"At least, that's what the doctor told me. But you gotta take what doctors tell you with a grain of salt. When I was in high school it scared the crap out of me, thinking I might, when I didn't know what I was doing, bash one of my classmates on the head with a hammer. I mean, when you're in high school you still don't know who you are, right? It's like you're living in some pipe underground. Add the pain of memory loss to that and you can't stand it."

I nodded silently. He might be right.

"I pretty much stopped going to school because of all that," my girlfriend's brother went on. "The more I thought about it, the more frightened I got, and

I couldn't bring myself to go to school. My mom explained the situation to my teacher, and even though I had way too many absences, they made an exception for me and let me graduate. I imagine the school wanted to get rid of a problem student like me as soon as it could. But I didn't go on to college. My grades weren't so bad, and I could have gotten into some kind of college, but I didn't have the confidence to go out. Ever since then, I've been loafing around at home. I take the dog for a walk, but otherwise I hardly ever leave the house. These days I don't feel as panicky, or whatever. If things calm down a little more, I think maybe I'll start going to college."

He was silent then, and so was I. I had no idea what to say. I understood now why my girlfriend never wanted to talk about her brother.

"Thank you for reading that story to

me," he said. "'Spinning Gears' is pretty good. A dark story, for sure, but some of the writing really got to me. You sure you don't want any coffee? It'll just take a minute."

"No, I'm fine, really. I'd better be going soon."

He glanced again at the clock on the wall. "Why don't you wait till twelve-thirty, and if nobody's back by then you can leave. I'll be in my room upstairs, so you can see yourself out. No need to worry about me."

I nodded.

"Is it interesting, going out with Sayoko?" my girlfriend's brother asked me one more time.

I nodded. "It's interesting."

"What part?"

"How there's so much about her I don't know," I replied. A very honest answer, I think.

"Hmm," he said, mulling it over. "Now that you mention it, I can see that. She's my kid sister, blood related, the same genes and all, and we've been living together under the same roof since she was born, but there are still tons of things I don't understand about her. I don't get her—how should I put it? What makes her tick? So I'd like it if you could understand those things for me. Though there may be things it's best not to try to figure out."

Coffee cup in hand, he rose from the armchair.

"Anyway, give it your best shot," my girlfriend's brother said. He fluttered his free hand at me and left the room.

"Thanks," I said.

At twelve-thirty, there was still no sign of anyone returning, so I went alone to the front door, slipped on my sneakers, and left. I walked past the pine forest to the station, jumped on the train, and went home. It was an oddly still and quiet Sunday autumn afternoon.

I got a call from my girlfriend after two p.m. "You were supposed to come next Sunday," she said. I wasn't totally convinced, but she was so clear about it that she was probably right. I must have messed up the days. I meekly apologized for going to her place a whole week early.

I didn't mention that while I was waiting for her to come home her brother and I had a conversation—maybe **conversation** wasn't the right word, since I basically just listened to him. I figured it was probably best not to say that I'd read Ryūnosuke Akutagawa's "Spinning Gears" to him, and that he had revealed to me that he had an illness with memory lapses. I had a kind of hunch, too, that he hadn't told my girlfriend anything about it. And if he hadn't, there wasn't any reason for me to.

Eighteen years later, I met her brother again. It was the middle of October. I was thirty-five then, living in Tokyo with my wife. After I graduated from college in Tokyo, I settled there. My work kept me busy, and I hardly ever went back to Kobe.

It was late afternoon, and I was walking up a hill in Shibuya to pick up a watch that was being repaired. I was heading along, lost in thought, when a man I'd passed turned and called out to me.

"Excuse me," he said. He had an unmistakable Kansai intonation. I stopped, turned around, and saw a man I didn't recognize. He looked a little older than me, and a tad taller. He had on a thick gray tweed jacket, a crew-neck, cream-colored cashmere sweater, and brown chinos. His hair was short, and he had the taut build of an athlete and a deep tan (a golf tan, it looked like). His features were unrefined, yet still attractive. Handsome, I suppose. I got the sense that this was a man who was pleased with his life. A well-bred person, was my guess.

"I don't recall your name, but weren't you my younger sister's boyfriend for a while?" he said.

I studied his face again. But I had no memory of it.

"Your younger sister?"

"Sayoko," he said. "I think you guys were in the same class in high school."

My eyes came to rest on a small tomato-sauce stain on the front of his cream-colored sweater. He was neatly dressed, and that one tiny stain struck me as out of place. And then it hit me—the twenty-one-year old brother with sleepy eyes and a loose-necked navy-blue sweater sprinkled with bread crumbs. Old habits die hard. Those kinds of inclinations, or habits, don't seem to ever change.

"I remember now," I said. "You're Sayoko's older brother. We met one time at your home, didn't we?"

"Right you are. You read Akutagawa's 'Spinning Gears' to me."

I laughed. "But I'm surprised you could pick me out in this crowd. We only met once, and it was so long ago."

"I'm not sure why, but I never forget a face. Plus, you don't seem to have changed at all."

"But you've changed quite a lot," I said. "You look so different now."

"Well—a lot of water under the bridge," he said, smiling. "As you know, things were pretty complicated for me for a while."

"How is Sayoko doing?" I asked.

He cast a troubled look to one side,

breathed in slowly, then exhaled. As if measuring the density of the air around him.

"Instead of standing here in the street, why don't we go somewhere where we can sit down and talk? If you're not busy, that is," he said.

"I have nothing pressing," I told him.

"SAYOKO PASSED AWAY," he said quietly. We were in a nearby coffee shop, seated across a plastic table from each other.

"Passed away?"

"She died. Three years ago."

I was speechless. I felt as if my tongue were swelling up inside my mouth. I tried to swallow the saliva that had built up, but couldn't.

The last time I'd seen Sayoko she was

twenty and had just gotten her driver's license, and she drove the two of us to the top of Mt. Rokko, in Kobe, in a white Toyota Crown hardtop that belonged to her father. Her driving was still a bit awkward, but she looked elated as she drove. Predictably, the radio was playing a Beatles song. I remember it well. "Hello, Goodbye." **You say goodbye, and I say hello.** As I said before, their music was everywhere then, surrounding us like wallpaper.

I couldn't grasp the fact that she'd died and no longer existed in this world. I'm not sure how to put it—it seemed so surreal.

"How did she . . . die?" I asked, my mouth dry.

"She committed suicide," he said, as if carefully picking his words. "When she was twenty-six she married a colleague at the insurance company she worked at, then had two children, then took her life. She was just thirty-two."

"She left behind children?"

My former girlfriend's brother nodded. "The older one is a boy, the younger a girl. Her husband's taking care of them. I visit them every once in a while. Great kids."

I still had trouble following the reality of it all. My former girlfriend had killed herself, leaving behind two small children?

"Why did she do it?"

He shook his head. "Nobody knows why. She didn't act like she was troubled or depressed. Her health was good, things seemed good between her and her husband, and she loved her kids. And she didn't leave behind a note or anything. Her doctor had prescribed sleeping pills, and she saved them up and took them all at once. So it does seem as though she was planning to kill herself. She wanted to die, and for six months she stashed away the medicine bit by bit. It wasn't just a sudden impulse."

I was silent for quite a while. And so was he. Each of us lost in our own thoughts.

On that day, in a café at the top of Mt. Rokko, my girlfriend and I broke up. I was going to a college in Tokyo and had fallen in love with a girl there. I came right out and confessed all this, and she, saying barely a word, grabbed her handbag, stood up, and hurried out of the café, without so much as a glance back.

I had to take the cable car down the mountain alone. She must have driven that white Toyota Crown home. It was a gorgeous, sunny day, and I remember I could see all of Kobe through the window of the gondola. It was an amazing view. But this was no longer the city I used to know so well.

That was the last time I ever saw Sayoko. She went on to college, got a job at a major insurance company, married one of her colleagues, had two children, saved up sleeping pills, and took her own life.

I would have broken up with her sooner or later. But, still, I have very fond memories of the years we spent together. She was my first girlfriend, and I liked her a lot. She was the person who taught me about the female body. We experienced all sorts of new things together, and shared some wonderful times, the kind that are possible only when you're in your teens.

It's hard for me to say this now, but she never rang that special bell inside my ears. I listened as hard as I could, but never once did it ring. Sadly. The girl I knew in Tokyo was the one who did it for me. This isn't something you can choose freely, according to logic or morality.

Either it happens or it doesn't. When it does, it happens of its own accord, in your consciousness or in a spot deep in your soul.

"You know," my former girlfriend's brother said, "it never crossed my mind, not once, that Sayoko would commit suicide. Even if everybody in the whole world had killed themselves, I figured—wrongly, it turns out—she'd still be standing, alive and well. I couldn't see her as the type to be disillusioned or have some darkness hidden away inside. Honestly, I thought she was a bit shallow. I never paid much attention to her, and the same was true for her when it came to me, I think. Maybe we just weren't on the same wavelength . . . Actually, I got along better with my other sister. But now I feel as though I did something awful to Sayoko, and it pains me. Maybe I never really knew her. Never understood a thing about her. Maybe I was too preoccupied with my own life. Perhaps somebody like me didn't have the strength to save her life, but I should have been able to understand something about her, even if it wasn't much. **Whatever it was** that led her to die. It's hard to bear now. I was so arrogant, so self-centered, and it hurts so much I can't stand it."

There was nothing I could say. I probably hadn't understood her at all, either. Like him, I'd been too preoccupied with my own life.

My former girlfriend's brother said, "In that story you read me back then, Akutagawa's 'Spinning Gears,' there was a part about how a pilot breathes in the air way up in the sky and then can't stand breathing the air back here on earth anymore . . . 'Airplane disease,' they called it. I don't know if that's a real disease or not, but I still remember those lines."

"Did you get over that condition where your memory flies away sometimes?" I asked him. I think I wanted to change the subject away from Sayoko.

"Oh, right. That," he said, narrowing his eyes a bit. "It's kind of weird, but that just spontaneously went away. It's a genetic disorder and it should have gotten worse over time, the doctor said, but it just up and vanished, as if I'd never had it. As if an evil spirit had been expelled."

"I'm glad to hear that," I said. And I really was.

"It happened not long after that time I met you. After that, I never experienced that kind of memory loss, not even once. I felt calmer, I was able to enter a halfway-decent college, graduate, and then take over my dad's business. Things took a detour for a few years there, but now I'm just living an ordinary life."

"I'm glad to hear that," I repeated. "So you didn't wind up bashing your father over the head with a hammer."

"You remember some dumb things, too, don't you," he said, and laughed out loud. "Still, you know, I don't come to Tokyo on business very often, and it seems strange to bump into you like this in this huge city. I can't help but feel that something brought us together."

"For sure," I said.

"So how about you? Have you been living in Tokyo all this time?"

"I got married right after I graduated from college," I told him, "and have been living here in Tokyo ever since. I'm making a living of sorts as a writer now."

"A writer?"

"Yeah. After a fashion."

"Well, you were really great at reading aloud," he said. "It might be a burden to you for me to tell you this, but I think Sayoko always liked you best of all."

I didn't reply. And my ex-girlfriend's brother didn't say anything more.

And so we said goodbye. I went to get my watch, which had been repaired, and my former girlfriend's older brother slowly set off down the hill to Shibuya station. His tweed-jacketed figure was swallowed up in the afternoon crowd.

I never saw him again. Chance had brought us together a second time. With nearly twenty years between encounters, in cities three hundred miles apart, we'd sat, a table between us, sipping coffee and talking over a few things. But these weren't subjects you just chatted about over coffee. There was something more significant in our talk, something that seemed meaningful to us, in the act of living out our lives. Still, it was merely a hint, delivered by chance. There was nothing to link us together in a more essential or organic way. [Question: What elements in the lives of these two were symbolically suggested by their meeting again and their conversation?] I never saw that lovely young girl again, either, the one who was holding the LP **With the Beatles**. Sometimes I wonder—is she still hurrying down that dimly lit high school hallway in 1964, the hem of her skirt fluttering as she goes? Sixteen even now, holding that wonderful album cover with the half-lit photo of John, Paul, George, and Ringo, clutching it tightly as though her life depended on it.

CONFESSIONS OF A

SHINAGAWA MONKEY

MET THE ELDERLY MONKEY in a small Japanese-style inn in a hot springs in Gunma Prefecture, some five years ago. The inn was rustic, or, more precisely, decrepit. It was barely hanging on and I just happened to spend a night there.

I was traveling around, wherever the spirit led me, and when I arrived at the hot springs town and got off the train, it was already past seven p.m. Autumn was nearly over, the sun had long since set, and the place was enveloped in that special navy-blue darkness specific to mountainous areas. A cold, biting wind blew down from the peaks, sending fist-sized leaves rustling down the street.

I walked through the central part of the hot springs town searching for a place to stay, but none of the decent inns would take guests after the dinner hour had passed. I stopped by five or six places, but they all turned me down, and finally, in a deserted area outside town, I ran across an inn that would take me that didn't include a dinner charge. It was a totally desolate-looking lodging, a ramshackle place that might best be called a flophouse. The inn had seen many years go by, but it lacked all the charm you might expect from a quaint lodging of its age. Mismatched fittings here and there were ever so slightly slanted, as if slapdash repairs had been made. I doubted that it would make it through the next earthquake, and I could only hope that no tremblor would hit that day, or the next.

They didn't serve dinner, but breakfast was included, and the fee for one night was incredibly cheap. Inside the entrance was a simple reception desk, behind which sat a completely hairless old man—devoid even of eyebrows—who took my payment for one night in advance. The lack of eyebrows made the old man's largish eyes seem to glisten bizarrely, glaringly. There was a large brown cat, equally ancient, sacked out on a floor cushion beside him. Something must have been wrong with its nose, for it snored louder than any cat I'd ever heard. Occasionally the rhythm of its snores fitfully missed a beat. Everything in this inn seemed to be old, ancient, and falling apart.

The room I was shown to was small,

like the little storage area where they keep futon bedding. The light on the ceiling was dim, and the flooring under the tatami creaked ominously with each step. But it was too late to be particular. I told myself I should be happy enough to have a roof over my head and a futon to sleep on.

I put my large shoulder bag, my only luggage, down on the floor and set off for town (this wasn't exactly the type of room I wanted to lounge around in). I went into a nearby soba noodle shop and had a simple dinner. There weren't any other restaurants open, so it was that place or nothing. I had a beer, some bar snacks, and some hot soba. The soba was mediocre, the soup lukewarm, but again, I wasn't about to complain. It certainly beat going to bed on an empty stomach. After I left the soba shop, I thought I'd buy some snacks and a small bottle of whiskey, but couldn't find a convenience store. It was after eight, and the only places open were the little shooting-gallery stalls typically found in hot springs towns. So I hoofed it back to the inn, changed into a **yukata**, and went downstairs to take a bath.

Compared to the shabby building and facilities, the hot springs bath at the inn was surprisingly wonderful. The steaming bathwater was a thick green color, not watered down, the sulfur odor more pungent than anything I'd ever experienced, and I soaked there, warming myself to the bone. There were no other bathers (I had no idea if there were even any people staying at the place besides me), and I was able to enjoy a long, leisurely soak. After a while I felt a little light-headed and got out to cool off. Then got back into the tub. Maybe this shoddy-looking little inn was a good choice after all, I figured. It was certainly more peaceful than bathing with some noisy tour group like in the larger inns.

I WAS SOAKING IN THE BATH for the third time when the monkey slid open the door with a clatter and came inside. "Excuse me," he said in a low voice. It took me a while to realize that this was a monkey. All the thick, hot water had made left me a little dazed, and I'd never expected to hear a monkey speak, so I couldn't quickly make the connection between what I was seeing and the fact that this was an actual monkey. My brain felt scattered as I gazed through the steam, uncomprehendingly, at the monkey, who slid the glass door closed behind him. He straightened up the little buckets that lay strewn about and stuck a thermometer into the bath to check the temperature. He gazed intently at the dial on the thermometer, his eyes narrowed, like a bacteriologist isolating some new strain of pathogen.

"How is the bath?" the monkey asked me.

"It's very nice. Thank you," I said. My voice reverberated densely, softly, in the steam. My voice sounded almost mythological. It didn't sound like it came from me, but rather like an echo from the past returning from deep in the forest. And that echo was . . . hold on a second. What was a **monkey** doing here? And why was he speaking in a human language?

"Shall I scrub your back for you?" the monkey asked, his voice again low. He had the clear, alluring voice of a doo-wop baritone. Not at all what you would expect. But nothing was odd about his voice, and if you closed your eyes and listened, you'd think it was an ordinary person speaking.

"Yes, thanks," I replied. It wasn't like I was sitting there, hoping someone would come and scrub my back, but I was afraid if I turned him down, he might think I was dead set against having a monkey ever scrub me down. It was a kind gesture on his part, I figured, and I certainly didn't want to hurt his feelings. So I slowly rose up out of the tub, plunked myself down on a little wooden platform, and turned my back to the monkey.

The monkey didn't have any clothes on. Which of course was usually the case for a monkey, so it didn't strike me as odd. The monkey seemed to be fairly old, and had a lot of white mixed in with his hair. He brought over a small towel, rubbed soap in it, and with a practiced hand gave my back a good scrubbing.

"It's gotten very cold these days, hasn't it," the monkey commented.

"That it has."

"Before long this place will be covered in snow. And then they'll have to shovel snow from the roofs, no easy task, believe you me."

There was a brief pause, and I jumped in. "So you can speak human language?"

"I can indeed," the monkey briskly replied. He was probably asked that a lot. "I was raised by humans, and before I knew it, I was able to speak. I lived for quite a long time in Tokyo, in Shinagawa."

"What part of Shinagawa?"

"Around Gotenyama."

"That's a nice area."

"Yes, as you're aware, it's a very pleasant place to live in. Nearby is the Gotenyama Gardens, and I enjoyed the natural scenery there."

Our conversation took a time out

at this point. The monkey continued briskly scrubbing my back (which felt great), and all the while I tried to puzzle all this out rationally. A monkey raised in Shinagawa? The Gotenyama Gardens? Fluent in human speech? How was that possible? This was a **monkey**, for goodness' sake. A monkey, and nothing else.

"I live in Minato-ku," I said, which was basically a meaningless statement.

"We were almost neighbors, then," the monkey said in a friendly tone.

"What kind of person raised you in Shinagawa?" I asked.

"My master was a college professor. He specialized in physics, and held a chair at Tokyo Gakugei University."

"Quite an intellectual, then."

"He certainly was. He loved music more than anything, particularly the music of Bruckner and Richard Strauss. Thanks to which I developed a fondness for that music myself. I heard it all the time since I was little. Picked up a knowledge of it without even realizing it, you could say."

"You enjoy Bruckner?"

"Yes. His Seventh Symphony. I always find the third movement particularly uplifting."

"I often listen to his Ninth Symphony," I chimed in. Another pretty meaningless statement.

"Yes, that's truly lovely music," the monkey said.

"So that professor taught you language?"

"He did. He didn't have any children, and perhaps to compensate for that, he trained me fairly strictly whenever he had time. He was very patient, a person who valued order and regularity above all. He was a serious person whose favorite saying was that the repetition of accurate facts was the true road to wisdom.

His wife was a quiet, sweet person, and was always kind to me. They got along well, and I hesitate to mention this to an outsider, but believe me, their nighttime activities could be quite intense."

"Really," I said.

The monkey finally finished scrubbing my back. "Thanks for your patience," he said, and bowed his head.

"Thank **you**," I said. "It really felt good. So, do you work here at this inn?"

"I do. They've been kind enough to let me work here. The larger, more upscale inns wouldn't ever hire a monkey. But they're always shorthanded around here, and if you can make yourself useful, they don't care whether you're a monkey or whatever. Being a monkey, the pay is minimal, and they only let me work where I mostly stay out of sight. Straightening up the bath, cleaning, things of this sort. Since most guests would be shocked if a monkey served them tea and so on. Working in the kitchen's out, too, since you'd run into issues with the Food Sanitation Law."

"Have you worked here a long time?" I asked.

"It's been about three years."

"But you must have gone through all sorts of things before you settled down here?"

The monkey gave a brisk nod. "Very true."

I hesitated, but then asked him, "If you don't mind, could you tell me more about your background?"

The monkey considered this, and then said, "Yes, that would be fine. It might not be as interesting as you expect, but I'm off work at ten and I could stop by your room after. Would that be convenient?"

"Certainly," I replied. "I'd be grateful if you could bring some beer then."

"Understood. Some cold beers it is. Would Sapporo be all right?"

"That would be fine. So, you drink beer?"

"A little bit, yes."

"Then please bring two large bottles."

"Certainly. If I understand correctly, you are staying in the Araiso suite on the second floor?"

That's right, I said.

"It's a little strange, though, don't you think?" the monkey said. "An inn in the mountains with a room named Araiso— 'Rugged Shore.'" He chuckled. I'd never in my life seen a monkey laugh before. But I guess monkeys do laugh, and even cry, at times. I shouldn't have been surprised, since he talked, too.

"By the way, do you have a name?" I asked.

"No, no name, per se. But everyone calls me the 'Shinagawa monkey.'"

The monkey slid open the glass door to the bath, turned, and gave a polite bow, then slowly slid the door shut.

IT WAS A LITTLE PAST TEN when the monkey came to the Araiso suite, bearing a tray with two large bottles of beer. (Like he said, I had no clue why they'd name the room "Rugged Shore"—Japanese inns did tend to give names to each of their rooms, but still, it was a seedy-looking room, more like a storage closet, with nothing whatsoever to conjure up any element of that name.) Besides the beer, the tray had a bottle opener, two glasses, plus some snacks—dried, seasoned squid and a bag of Kakipi crunchy snacks—small pieces of rice crackers with peanuts. Typical bar snacks. This was one attentive monkey.

· · · ·

THE MONKEY WAS DRESSED NOW, in a thick, long-sleeved shirt with I♥NY printed on it, and gray sweatpants, probably some hand-me-down kid's clothes.

There wasn't a table in the room, so we sat down, side by side, on thin **zabuton** cushions, and leaned back against the wall. The monkey used the opener to pop the cap on one of the beers and poured out two glasses. Silently we clinked our glasses together in a little toast.

"Thanks for the drinks," the monkey said, and happily gulped back the cold beer. I drank some as well. Honestly, it felt odd to be seated next to a monkey, sharing a beer, but I guess you get used to it.

"A beer after work can't be beat," the monkey said, wiping his mouth with the hairy back of his hand. "But being a monkey, the opportunities to have a beer like this are few and far between."

"Do you live here, at your workplace?"

"Yes, there's a room, sort of an attic, where they let me sleep. There are mice from time to time, so it's hard to relax there, but I'm a monkey so I have to be thankful to have a bed to sleep in and three square meals a day . . . Not that it's paradise or anything."

The monkey had finished his first glass, so I poured him another.

"Much obliged," he said politely.

"Have you lived, not just with humans, but with your own kind? With other monkeys, I mean?" I asked. There were so many things I wanted to ask him.

"Yes, several times," the monkey answered, his face clouding over a little. The wrinkles beside his eyes formed deep folds. "For various reasons I was driven out, forcibly, from Shinagawa and released in Takasakiyama, the area down south famous for its monkey park. I thought at first I could live peaceably there, but things didn't work out that way. The other monkeys are my dear compatriots, don't get me wrong, but having been raised in a human household, by the professor and his wife, I just couldn't express my feelings well to them. We had little in common, and communication wasn't easy. 'You talk funny,' they told me, and sort of made fun of me and bullied me. The female monkeys would giggle when they looked at me. Monkeys are extremely sensitive to the most minute differences. They found the way I acted comical, and it annoyed them, even made them irritated sometimes. It got harder for me to stay with them, so eventually I went off on my own. Turned into a **rogue monkey**, in other words."

"It must have been lonely for you."

"Indeed it was. Nobody protected me, and I had to scrounge for food on my own and somehow survive. But the worst thing was not having anyone to communicate with. I couldn't talk with monkeys, or with humans. Isolation like that is heartrending. Takasakiyama is full of human visitors, but that didn't mean I could just start up a conversation with whomever I happened to run across. Do that and there'd be hell to pay. The upshot was I wound up sort of neither here nor there, an isolated monkey, not part of human society, not part of the monkeys' world. It was a harrowing existence."

"And you couldn't listen to Bruckner, either."

"True. That's not part of my world anymore," the Shinagawa monkey said, and drank some more beer. I studied his face, but since it was red to begin with, I didn't notice it turning any redder. I figured this monkey could hold his liquor. Or maybe with monkeys you can't tell from their faces when they're drunk.

"The other thing that really tormented me was relations with females."

"I see," I said. "And by relations with females you mean—"

"To be brief, I didn't feel a speck of sexual desire for female monkeys. I had a lot of opportunities to be with them, but never really felt like it."

"So female monkeys didn't turn you on, even though you're a monkey yourself?"

"Yes. That's exactly right. It's embarrassing, but honestly, before I knew it, I could only love human females."

I was silent and drained my glass of beer. I opened the bag of crunchy snacks and grabbed a handful. "That could lead to some real problems, I would think."

"Yes, some real problems indeed. Me being a monkey, after all, there's no way

I could expect human females to respond to my desires. Plus it runs counter to genetics."

I waited for him to go on. The monkey rubbed hard behind his ear and finally continued.

"So because of all this I had to find another method of ridding myself of these unfulfilled desires."

"What do you mean by 'another method'?"

The monkey frowned deeply. His red face turned a bit darker.

"You may not believe me," the monkey said. "You probably **won't** believe me, I should say. But I started stealing the names of women I fell for."

"Stealing names?"

"Correct. I'm not sure why, but I seem to have been born with a special talent for it. If I feel like it, I can steal somebody's name and make it my own."

A wave of confusion hit me again.

"I'm not sure I get it," I said. "When you say you steal a person's name, you mean that person completely loses their name?"

"No. They don't totally lose their name. What I steal is **part** of their name, a fragment. But when I do, the name becomes insubstantial, that much lighter than before. Like when the sun clouds over and your shadow on the ground gets that much paler. And depending on the person, they might not be aware of the loss. They just have a sense that something's a little off."

"But some do clearly realize it, right? That a part of their name's been stolen?"

"Yes, of course. Sometimes they find that they can't remember their name. Quite inconvenient, a real bother, as you might imagine. And they don't even recognize their name for what it is. In some cases, they suffer through something close to an identity crisis. And it's all my fault, since I stole that person's name. I feel very sorry about that. I often feel the weight of a guilty conscience bearing down on me. I know it's wrong, yet I can't stop myself. I'm not trying to excuse my actions, but my dopamine levels force me to do that. Like there's a voice telling me, **Hey, go ahead, steal the name. It's not like it's illegal or anything**."

I folded my arms and studied the monkey. **Dopamine?** Finally, I spoke up. "And the names you steal are only those of the women you love or sexually desire. Do I have that right?"

"Exactly. I don't randomly steal just anybody's name."

"How many people's names have you stolen?"

With a serious expression the monkey totaled it up on his fingers. As he counted, he was muttering something. He looked up. "Seven in all. I stole seven women's names."

Was this a lot, or not so many? Who could say?

"So how do you go about stealing names?" I asked. "If you don't mind telling me?"

"It's mostly by willpower. Power of concentration, psychic energy. But that's not enough. I need something with the person's name actually written on it. An ID is ideal. A driver's license, student ID, insurance card, or passport. Things of this sort. A name tag will work, too. Anyway, I need to get hold of an actual object like that. Mostly I steal them. Stealing is the only way. As a monkey I'm pretty skilled at sneaking into people's rooms when they're out. I scout around for something with their name on it and take it back with me."

"So you use that object with the woman's name on it, along with your willpower, and steal their name."

"Precisely. I stare at the name written there for a long time, focusing my emotions, absorbing the name of the person I love. It takes a lot of time, and is mentally and physically exhausting. I get completely engrossed in it, and somehow am able to pull it off—a part of the woman becomes a part of me. And my affection and desire, which up until then had no outlet, are safely satisfied."

"So there's nothing physical involved?"

The monkey nodded sharply. "I know I'm just a monkey, but I never do anything unseemly. I make the name of the woman I love a part of me—that's enough for me. I agree it's a bit perverted, but it's also a completely pure, platonic act. I simply possess a great love for that name inside me, secretly. Like a gentle breeze wafting over a meadow."

"Hmm," I said, impressed. "I guess you could even call that the ultimate form of romantic love."

"Agreed. It may well be the ultimate form of romantic love. But it's also the ultimate form of loneliness. Like two sides of a coin. The two extremes are stuck together, and can never be separated."

Our conversation came to a halt here, and the monkey and I silently drank our beer, snacking on the Kakipi and dried squid.

"Have you stolen anyone's name recently?" I asked.

The monkey shook his head. He grabbed some of the stiff hair on his arm, as if making sure he was, indeed, an actual monkey. "No, I haven't stolen anyone's name recently. After I came to this town,

I made up my mind to stop that kind of misconduct. Thanks to which, the soul of this wee little monkey has found a measure of peace. I treasure the names of the seven women in my heart, and live a quiet, tranquil life."

"I'm glad to hear it," I said.

"I know this is quite forward of me, but I was wondering if you'd be kind enough to allow me to give my own personal opinion on the subject of love."

"Of course," I said.

The monkey blinked widely several times. His long eyelashes waved up and down like palm fronds in the breeze. He took a big, slow breath, the kind of deep breath a long jumper takes before he starts to run.

"I believe that love is the indispensable fuel that allows us to go on living. Someday that love may end. Or it may never amount to anything. But even if love fades away, even if it's unrequited, you can still hold on to the memory of having loved someone, of having fallen in love with someone. And that's a valuable source of warmth. Without that heat source a person's heart—and a monkey's heart, too—would turn into a bitterly cold, barren wasteland. A place where not a ray of sunlight falls, where the wildflowers of peace, the trees of hope, have no chance to grow. I treasure the names of those seven beautiful women I loved here in my heart." At this, the monkey laid a palm on his chest. "I plan to use these memories as my own little fuel source I burn on cold nights to keep me warm as I live out what's left of my own personal life."

The monkey chuckled again, and lightly shook his head a few times.

"That's a strange way of putting it, isn't

it," he said. "**Personal** life. When I'm a monkey, not a **person**. Hee hee . . ."

IT WAS ELEVEN THIRTY when we finally finished drinking the two large bottles of beer. I should be going, the monkey said. "I started feeling so good I ran off at the mouth, I'm afraid. My apologies."

"No, I found it an interesting story," I said. Maybe **interesting** wasn't the right word. I mean, sharing a beer and chatting together with a monkey was a pretty unusual experience. Add to that the fact that this particular monkey loved Bruckner and stole women's names because he was driven to do so by sexual desire (or perhaps love), and **interesting** didn't begin to describe it. It was the most incredible thing I'd ever heard. But I didn't want to stir the monkey's emotions any more than necessary, so I chose this more calming, neutral expression.

As we said goodbye, I handed the monkey a ¥1,000 bill as a tip. "It's not much, but please buy yourself something good to eat."

At first the monkey refused, but I insisted and he finally accepted it. He folded the bill and carefully slipped it into the pocket of his sweatpants.

"It's very kind of you," he said. "You've listened to my absurd life story, treated me to beer, and now this kind gesture. I can't tell you how much I appreciate it."

The monkey put the empty beer bottles and glasses on the tray and carried it out of the room.

THE NEXT MORNING, I checked out of the inn and went back to Tokyo, but I didn't see the monkey anywhere. At the front desk, the creepy old man with no hair or eyebrows was nowhere to be seen, and neither was the aged cat with the nose issues. Instead, a fat, surly middle-aged woman was manning the front, and when I said I'd like to pay for the additional charges for last night's beer, she said, emphatically, that there were no incidental charges on my bill. All we have here is canned beer from the vending machine, she insisted. We never provide bottled beer.

Once again, I was confused. It felt like bits of reality and unreality were randomly changing places. But I had definitely shared two large bottles of Sapporo beer with the monkey as I listened to his life story.

I was going to bring up the monkey with the middle-aged woman, but decided against it. Maybe the monkey didn't really exist, and it was all an illusion, the product of a brain pickled after soaking too long in the hot springs. Or maybe what I had seen was a long, strange, realistic dream. So if I said something like "You have an employee who's an elderly monkey who can speak, right?" things might go sideways, and, worst-case scenario, they'd think I was insane. Another possibility was that the monkey was an off-the-books employee, and the inn couldn't mention it publicly, not wanting the tax office or health department to catch wind of it—a real possibility.

On the train ride back home, I mentally replayed everything the monkey had told me. I jotted down all the details, as best I could remember, in a notebook I used for work, thinking that when I got back to Tokyo I'd write down the whole thing from start to finish.

If the monkey really **did** exist—and that's the only way I could see it—I wasn't at all sure how much I should accept of what he had told me over beer. It was hard to judge it fairly. Was that really possible? To steal women's names and possess them yourself? Was this some unique ability that only the Shinagawa monkey was given? Maybe the monkey was a pathological liar. Who could say? Naturally I'd never heard of a monkey with mythomania before, but if a monkey could speak human language as skillfully as he did, it wouldn't be beyond the realm of possibility for him to also be a habitual liar.

I'd interviewed numerous people as part of my work, and had become pretty good at sniffing out who you could believe and who you couldn't. After someone talks for a while, you pick up some subtle hints and certain signals the man (or woman) sends out, and you get an intuitive sense of whether or not they're believable. And I just didn't get the feeling that what the Shinagawa monkey told me was a made-up story. The look in his eyes and his expression, the way he'd ponder things every once in a while, his pauses, gestures, the way he'd get stuck for words— nothing about it seemed artificial or forced. And above all was the total, even painful, honesty of his confession.

My relaxed solo journey over, I returned to the whirlwind routine of the city. Even without any major work-related assignments, somehow as I get older I find myself busier than ever. And time seems to steadily speed up. In the end I never told anyone about the Shinagawa monkey, or wrote anything about him. Why try if no one would ever believe me? People would only end up saying I was just "making up stuff again." I also couldn't figure out what format to use.

It was way too bizarre to write about it as if it were real, and as long as I couldn't provide proof—proof, that is, that the monkey actually existed—no one would ever buy it. That said, if I wrote about it as fiction, it lacked a clear focus, or a point. I could well imagine, even before I started writing about it, my editor's puzzled expression after reading the manuscript, and the question that would follow: "I hesitate to ask you, since you're the author, but—what's the theme of this story supposed to be?"

Theme? Can't say there is one. It's just about an old monkey who speaks human language, in a tiny town in Gunma Prefecture, who scrubs guests' backs in the hot springs, enjoys cold beer, falls in love with human women, and steals their names. Where's the theme in that? Or moral?

And as time passed, the memory of

that hot springs town began to fade. No matter how vivid memories may be, they can't win out against the power of time.

BUT NOW, five years later, I've decided to write about it, based on the notes I scribbled down in my notebook back then. All because of something that happened recently that got me thinking. If that incident hadn't taken place, I might well not be writing this.

I had a work-related appointment in the coffee lounge of a hotel in Akasaka. The person I was meeting was an editor of a travel magazine. She was a very attractive woman, around thirty or so, petite, with long hair, a lovely complexion, and large, fetching eyes. She was also quite an able editor. And still single. We'd worked together quite a few times, and got along well. After we'd taken care of work, we sat back and chatted over coffee for a while.

Her cell phone rang, and she looked at me apologetically. I motioned to her to take the call. She checked the incoming number and answered it. It seemed to be about some reservation she'd made. At a restaurant, maybe, or hotel, or air flight. Something along those lines. She talked for a while, checking her pocket planner, and then shot me a troubled look.

"I'm very sorry," she said to me in a small voice, hand covering the speaker. "This is a weird question, I know, but what's my name?"

I gasped, but, as casually as I could, I told her her full name. She nodded and relayed this to the person on the other end of the phone. She hung up, and apologized to me.

"I'm so sorry about that. All of a sudden

I just couldn't remember my name. I'm so embarrassed."

"Does that happen sometimes?" I asked.

She seemed to hesitate, but finally nodded. "Yes, it's happening a lot these days. I just can't recall my name. Like I've blacked out or something."

"Do you forget other things too? Like you can't remember your birthday, or telephone number, or a PIN?"

She shook her head decisively. "No, not at all. I've always had a good memory. I know all my friends' birthdays by heart. I haven't forgotten anyone else's name, not even once. But still, sometimes I can't remember my own name. I can't figure it out. After a couple minutes my memory comes back, but that couple of minutes is totally inconvenient, and I panic, like I'm no longer myself anymore."

I nodded silently.

"Do you think it's a sign of early-onset Alzheimer's?" she asked.

I sighed. "Medically, I don't know, but when did it start—those symptoms where you suddenly forget your name?"

She squinted and thought about it. "About a half a year ago, I think. I remember it was when I went to enjoy the cherry blossoms, and I couldn't recall my name. That was the first time."

"This might be an odd thing to ask, but did you lose anything at that time? Some sort of ID, like a driver's license, a passport, an insurance card?"

She pursed her lip, lost in thought for a while, then replied.

"You know, now that you mention it, I did lose my driver's license back then. It was lunchtime and I was sitting on a park bench, taking a break, and I put my handbag right next to me on the bench. I was redoing my lipstick with my compact, and when I looked over next, the handbag was gone. I couldn't understand it. I'd only looked away from the handbag for a second, and didn't sense anyone nearby, or hear any footsteps. I looked around, but I was alone. It was a quiet park, and I'm sure if somebody had come to steal my bag I would have noticed it."

I waited for her to go on.

"But that's not all that was strange. That same afternoon I got a call from the police saying my handbag had been found. It had been set outside a police box near the park. Nothing else was missing—the cash was still inside, as were my credit cards, ATM card, and cell phone. All there, untouched. Only my driver's license was gone. That was the only thing taken from my purse. It seemed unthinkable, and the policeman was quite surprised. They don't take the cash, only the license, and leave the bag right outside a police box?"

I sighed quietly, but said nothing.

"This was the end of March. Right away I went to the Motor Vehicles office in Samezu and had them issue a new license. The whole incident was pretty weird, but fortunately there wasn't any real harm done. And Samezu's near work, so it didn't take much time."

"Samezu is in Shinagawa, isn't it?"

"That's right. It's in Higashioi. My company's in Takanawa, so it's a quick taxi ride," she said. She turned a doubtful look at me. "Do you think there's a connection? Between me not remembering my name and losing my license?"

I quickly shook my head. I couldn't exactly bring up the story of the Shinagawa monkey here. If I did, she might wangle his whereabouts from me, and head off to that inn to confront him face-to-face. And grill him about what had happened.

"No, I don't think there's a connection," I said. "It just sort of popped into my head. Since it involves your name."

She still looked unconvinced. I knew it was risky, but there was one more vital question I had to ask.

"By the way, have you seen any monkeys lately?"

"Monkeys?" she asked. "You mean, like the animals?"

"Yes, real live monkeys," I said.

She shook her head. "I don't think I've seen a monkey for years. Not in a zoo, or anywhere else."

WAS THE SHINAGAWA MONKEY back to his old tricks? Or was another monkey using his MO to commit these crimes?

(A copycat monkey!) Or was something else, other than a monkey, responsible?

I really didn't want to think the Shinagawa monkey was back to stealing names. He'd told me, quite matter-of-factly, that holding seven women's names tucked inside him was plenty, and that he was happy simply living out his remaining years quietly in that little hot springs town. And he seemed to mean it. But maybe that monkey had a chronic psychological condition, one that reason alone couldn't hold in check. And maybe his illness, and his dopamine, was urging him to **just do it!** And perhaps all that brought him back to his old haunts in Shinagawa, back to his former, pernicious habits.

Maybe I'll try it myself sometime. On sleepless nights, that random, fanciful thought comes to me sometimes. I'll filch the ID or name tag of a woman I love, set a laser-like focus on it, gather her name inside me, and possess a part of her all to myself. What would that feel like? No. That'll never happen. I've never been deft with my hands, and would never be able to swipe something that belonged to someone else. Even if that **something** had no physical form, and stealing it wasn't against the law.

Extreme love, extreme loneliness. Ever since then, whenever I listen to a Bruckner symphony, I ponder that Shinagawa monkey's **personal life**. I picture the elderly monkey in that tiny hot springs town, in the attic of a rundown inn, wrapped up in a thin quilt, asleep. And I think of the snacks—the Kakipi and dried squid—we enjoyed as we drank beer together, propped up against the wall.

I haven't seen the beautiful travel magazine editor since then, so I have no idea what happened with her name. I hope it didn't cause her any real hardship. She was blameless, after all. Nothing about it was her fault. I do feel bad about it, but I still can't bring myself to tell her about the Shinagawa monkey.

CARNAVAL

OF ALL THE WOMEN I've known until now, she was the ugliest. But this might not be a fair way of putting it. I've known lots of women whose looks were uglier. I think I'm on safe ground, though, in saying that among the women I've been close with in my life—those who have put down roots in the soil of my memory—she was indeed the ugliest. I could use a euphemism, of course, and say **least beautiful** in place of **ugly**, which should be easier for readers, especially women readers, to accept. But I've decided to go with the more straightforward (and somewhat brutal) term instead here, for this captures more the essence of who she really was.

I'm going to call her F*. There are a couple of reasons it wouldn't be appropriate to reveal her real name. Incidentally, her real name has nothing to do with either F or with *.

Perhaps F* might read this story somewhere. She often told me she was only interested in works by living women writers, but it's not impossible that she might run across these words. And if she did, she'd surely recognize herself here. Even if that happened, I seriously doubt that my saying "Of all the women I've known until now, she was the ugliest" would bother her much. For all I know, she might even find it amusing. She was more aware than anyone that her looks were far from appealing, or **ugly**, as I put it, and even enjoyed using this to her advantage.

I don't imagine there are many cases like this. First of all, there aren't that many ugly women who realize they're ugly, and those who do go on to take some pleasure in their ugliness are certainly a minuscule fraction. In that sense, I think she was **unique**. And it was that very **uniqueness** that drew people to her. Like a magnet attracts all sorts of metal to itself—some useful, some worthless.

TALKING ABOUT ugliness also means talking about beauty.

I know a few beautiful women, the kind that anyone would find lovely and charming. But to me those beautiful women, the majority of them at least, never seem able to truly, unconditionally, derive pleasure in being gorgeous. Kind of strange, I think. Women who are born beautiful are always the center of men's attention. Other women are jealous of them and they get coddled no end. People give them expensive presents, and they have their pick of men. So why don't they seem happier? Why do they sometimes even seem depressed?

What I've observed is that most of the beautiful women I know are dissatisfied, and irritated by tiny, inconsequential flaws—the kind inevitably found somewhere in any person's physical makeup. They obsess over these little details. Their big toes are too big, or their nails are weirdly off center, or their nipples aren't the same size. One gorgeous woman I know is convinced that her earlobes are too long, and always wears her hair long to hide them. I couldn't care less about the length of someone's earlobes (she showed me hers once and they struck me as perfectly normal). Maybe, though, all this stuff about earlobes was just a substitute, a way of expressing something else.

Compared to these women, isn't a woman who is not beautiful—who is even considered to be ugly—and yet enjoys that fact, a far happier person? No matter how beautiful a woman might be, she always has imperfections, and likewise no matter how ugly a woman might be, there's always a part of her that is beautiful. And they seem to freely revel in that part of themselves, unlike beautiful women. It's not a substitute for anything, or a metaphor.

This might sound like a banal opinion, but the world can turn upside down, depending on the way we look at it. The way a ray of sunshine falls on something can change shadow to light, or light to shadow. A positive becomes a negative, a negative a positive. I don't know if this is an essential part of the way the world works, or simply an optical illusion. But it's in that way that F* was a sort of trickster with light.

A FRIEND OF MINE first introduced me to her. I was just past fifty then, and she was about ten years younger. But for her, age didn't matter. Her looks surpassed any other personal factors. Age, height, the shape and size of one's breasts, let alone the shape of big toenails or the length of one's earlobes, all took a back seat to her spectacular lack of beauty.

I was at a concert in Suntory Hall when I ran across a male friend of mine having a glass of wine with F* during intermission. One of Mahler's symphonies was on the program that evening (I forget which one). The first half of the program featured Prokofiev's **Romeo and Juliet**. My friend introduced me to F* and the three of us had some wine and talked about Prokofiev's music. All of us had come alone to the concert and my friend just happened to run across her there too. People who go to concerts by themselves always share a sense of solidarity, albeit a small one.

Naturally, when I met F* my first thought was that this was one singularly ugly woman. She was so friendly and straightforward, though, that I was embarrassed by my initial reaction. I'm not sure how to put it exactly, but as we chatted, I grew accustomed to her looks. They no longer seemed to matter. She was a pleasant person, and a good talker, able to converse widely. Add to this a quick mind, and good taste in music. When the buzzer sounded ending the intermission, and then when we said goodbye, I thought if only she were good-looking, or at least if her looks were a **little better**, she'd be a very appealing woman.

But later on, I learned the hard way how shallow and superficial my thinking had been. It was precisely **because** of her unusual looks that she was able to effectively engage her powerful personality—her power to draw people in, you might put it. What I mean is, it was precisely the gap between her physical appearance and her refinement that created her own special brand of dynamism. And she was fully aware of that power, and was able to use it as needed.

It's next to impossible for me to describe exactly what it was about her looks that was so unappealing. No matter how I try to describe her, I'll never be able to convey to the reader the idiosyncrasies of her appearance. One thing I can say for sure, though, is this: you wouldn't be able to pinpoint any functional imperfections. So it wasn't like—this part's weird, or fix this part and she'd look a bit better. Yet combine them all and you wound up with an organically comprehensive ugliness. (It's an odd comparison, but the process reminds me of the birth of Venus.) And it's impossible for words or logic to explain that composite. Even supposing I could, it wouldn't mean much anyway. What we have there is a choice between two alternatives, and only two—we either wholly accept it, unconditionally, as something that **is what it is**, or we completely reject it. Like a take-no-prisoners type of war.

In the opening of **Anna Karenina**, Tolstoy wrote, "Happy families are all alike; every unhappy family is unhappy in its own way," and I think the same applies to women's faces in terms of beauty or ugliness. I believe (and please take this for what it is, just my personal view) that beautiful woman can be summed up by simply being "beautiful." Each one of them is carrying around a single beautiful, golden-haired monkey on her back. There might be a slight difference in the luster and shade of their fur, but the brilliance they share makes them all seem one and the same.

In contrast, ugly women each carry around their own individual version of a shaggy monkey. There are small, but significant, differences in their monkeys—how worn their fur is, where their fur has thinned out, how dirty they are. There's no brilliance at all, so unlike the golden-haired monkeys, our eyes are not dazzled by them.

The monkey that F* carried around on her back had a variety of expressions, and its fur—though never sparkling or shining—was a composite of several colors simultaneously. One's impression of that monkey changed drastically depending on the angle you viewed it from, as well as by the weather, the wind, direction, the time of day. To put it another way, the ugliness of her features was the result of a unique force that compressed unattractive elements of all shapes and sizes and assembled them together in one place. And her monkey had quietly settled down, very comfortably, and unhesitantly, on her back, as if every possible cause and effect had embraced at the very center of the world.

I was aware of all this, to some extent, the second time I met F*, though certainly still unable to articulate it. I knew it would take some time to understand her ugliness, and doing so would require intuition, philosophy, morality, and a bit of real-life experience. And that spending time with her would, at a certain point, lead to a sort of feeling of pride. It was pride at the fact that we'd somehow managed to grab hold of the requisite intuition, philosophy, morality, and life experience.

THE SECOND TIME I saw her was also at a concert hall, a smaller venue than Suntory Hall. It was a concert by a French female violinist. As I recall, she played sonatas by Franck and Debussy. She was an amazing musician, and these pieces were part of her favorite repertoire, but on that particular day she wasn't at her best. The two pieces by Kreisler she played for an encore, though, were quite charming.

I was outside the concert hall, waiting for a taxi, when she called to me from behind. F* was with a woman friend then, a small, slim, beautiful friend. F* herself was rather tall, just a bit shorter than I am.

"I know a nice place just down the street," she said. "Would you care to go have a glass of wine or something?"

Sounds good, I told her. The night was still young, and I was feeling some lingering frustration over the concert. I felt like having a glass or two of wine and talking with someone about fine music.

The three of us settled down in a small bistro in a nearby side street, ordered wine and some snacks, but her lovely friend soon got up to take a phone call. A family member had called telling her that her cat was sick. So then it was just F* and me. But I wasn't especially disappointed, since by this time I was starting to be interested in F*. She had excellent taste in clothes and wore an obviously high-end blue silk dress. The jewelry she wore was perfect, too. Simple, but the kind that caught your eye. It was then that I noticed she was wearing a wedding ring.

She and I talked about the concert. We agreed that the violinist hadn't been at her best. Maybe she wasn't feeling well, or had some pain in her fingers, or maybe she wasn't happy with the hotel room she'd been provided. But no doubt something was wrong. You're sure to run across those kinds of things when you attend concerts often enough.

We moved on to talking about the kinds of music we liked. We agreed that we both liked piano music the best. Of course we listened to opera, symphonies, and chamber music, but what we liked best was solo piano music. And strangely enough, there was a lot of overlap in our favorite pieces. Neither of us could get too enthusiastic for long about Chopin. At least it wasn't what we wanted to hear first thing in the morning. Mozart's piano music was beautiful, and charming, for sure, but frankly we'd grown tired of it. Bach's **The Well-Tempered Clavier** was amazing, but a bit too long to really focus on. You had to be in good physical shape to properly appreciate it. Beethoven's piano music sometimes struck us as overly serious, and (we believed) it had been dissected enough already, from every conceivable angle. Brahms's piano music was lovely to listen to on occasion, but exhausting if heard all the time. Not to mention often boring. And with Debussy and Ravel you had to carefully choose the time and place you heard them in, or else you couldn't fully appreciate their music.

Without a doubt, we decided, the

pinnacle of the piano repertoire was several Schubert sonatas, and the music of Schumann. Of all those, which one would you choose?

JUST ONE?

That's right, F* said, just one. The one piano piece you would take with you to a desert island.

Not an easy question. I had to give it some serious thought.

Schumann's **Carnaval**, I finally declared.

F* narrowed her eyes and gazed at me for a long time. She then rested her hands on the table, laced them together, and loudly cracked the knuckles. Exactly ten times. So loud that people at nearby tables glanced our way. It was a hard sound, like snapping a three-day-old baguette on your knee. There aren't that many people—men or women—who can crack their knuckles that loudly. I figured it out later, but loudly cracking her knuckles ten times was her habit when she was excited and enthusiastic. I didn't know that then, however, and wondered if something had upset her. Probably my choice of **Carnaval** was inappropriate. But there it was. The fact was, I've always loved the piece. Even if it made someone so angry that they wanted to punch me, I still wasn't going to lie about it.

"You're really going to go with **Carnaval**?" She frowned, raised one long finger, making sure of things. "As the one piece out of all piano pieces you'd take with you to a desert island?"

I felt unsure, now that she said this. In order to preserve Schumann's incoherent piano music, beautiful as a kaleidoscope, and somehow beyond the bounds of human intellect, was I really willing to chuck Bach's **Goldberg Variations** or

Well-Tempered Clavier? Beethoven's late piano sonatas, and his brave, and charming, Third Concerto?

A brief, heavy silence followed, while F* pushed her fists together hard a few times, as if checking how her hands were doing.

"You have wonderful taste," she finally said. "And I admire your courage. I'm with you. Schumann's **Carnaval** would be my choice too."

"Seriously?"

"Seriously. I've always loved it. I never get tired of it, no matter how many times I hear it."

We went on for some time discussing the piece. We ordered a bottle of Pinot Noir, and finished it as we talked. We became friends of a sort that evening. **Carnaval** buddies. Though this relationship only lasted about a half a year.

· · ·

SO WE MADE OUR OWN kind of two-member-only, private **Carnaval** Club. There was no reason that it had to be limited to just two, but it never exceeded that number. Since we never ran across anyone else as crazy about the piece as we were.

We listened to numerous records and CDs of performances of **Carnaval**, and if a pianist was including the piece in his concert, we did everything we could to attend together. According to my notebook (I took copious notes on each and every performance), we went to live performances of **Carnaval** by three separate pianists, and listened together to forty-two CDs and records of the piece. Afterward we'd cozily exchange opinions on them. Turns out that a lot of pianists, in all times and places, have recorded the piece, which seemed to be a popular part of their repertoire. For all that, we only found a handful of performances acceptable.

A performance could be technically flawless, but if the technique was not completely in sync with the music, **Carnaval** collapsed into nothing more than a mechanical finger exercise, and its appeal vanished. It was, indeed, very challenging to pull off the expression just right, beyond the abilities of your run-of-the-mill pianist. I won't name anyone, but not a few major pianists made recordings of fumbled performances, bereft of any charisma. And many other pianists avoided playing it altogether. (At least that's the only thing I can surmise.) Vladimir Horowitz loved Schumann's music and performed it throughout his career, but for some reason never made a proper recording of **Carnaval**. And the same can be said of Sviatoslav Richter. And I can't be the only person who would one day love to hear Martha Argerich perform the piece.

INCIDENTALLY, almost none of Schumann's contemporaries understood how wonderful his music was. Mendelssohn and Chopin, for instance, didn't think much of Schumann's piano music. Even Schumann's widow, Clara (one of the top pianists of her time), who devotedly played his music, secretly wished that he had focused on more standard-type operas or symphonies rather than this kind of whimsical composition. Basically, Schumann wasn't fond of classical forms like the sonata, and occasionally his pieces came across as rambling and starry-eyed. He moved away from the existing classical forms, which resulted in the birth of a new type of music, the Romantic school, but most of his contemporaries thought his work was eccentric, lacking a solid foundation and content. It was this bold eccentricity, however, that propelled the rise of Romantic music.

AT ANY RATE, during those six months the two of us listened to **Carnaval** every chance we got. That wasn't all we listened to, of course—Mozart and Brahms were on our menu from time to time—but whenever we met, we'd end up listening to a version of **Carnaval** and share our reactions to the performance. I was our little club's secretary, and noted down summaries of our opinions. She came to my house several times, but more often than not I went to hers, as she lived near the center of the city, while I was out in the suburbs. After hearing forty-two recorded versions of the piece, her number one choice was Arturo Benedetti Michelangeli's recording for Angel Records, and mine was Arthur Rubinstein's RCA recording. We carefully graded each and every disc we listened to, knowing of course that it really didn't amount to much. It was just an extra bit of fun thrown in. What was most important to us was talking about the music we loved, the feeling of almost aimlessly sharing something we were passionate about.

You'd think that a man seeing a woman ten years younger this frequently would cause some discord at home, but my wife didn't worry about her at all. I won't deny that F*'s unattractive looks played a major role in my wife's disinterest. She didn't have a bit of suspicion or doubt that F* and I might fall into a sexual relationship, a major benefit her looks afforded us. My wife just seemed to find us a pair of nerds. She wasn't into classical music herself, as most concerts bored her. My wife dubbed F* "your girlfriend." And sometimes, with a hint of sarcasm, "your lovely girlfriend."

I never met F*'s husband. (She didn't have any children). Maybe by coincidence, he was out whenever I visited her place, or else she specifically chose times he wouldn't be there. Or maybe he was out most of the time. Which it was, I couldn't say. While we're on the subject, I couldn't even tell for sure if she really had a husband. She never said a single thing about him, and as far as I recall, there wasn't a trace of a man anywhere about the place. That said, she had announced that she had a husband, and wore a sparkling gold wedding ring on the ring finger of her left hand.

She also never said a word about her past. She never mentioned where she was from, what kind of family she had, which schools she went to, or what kind of jobs she'd had. If I asked her about personal things, all I got back was vague innuendo or a wordless smile. All I did know about her was that she worked in some specialized field and had quite an affluent lifestyle. She lived in the trendy Daikanyama neighborhood in Tokyo, in an elegant three-bedroom condo in a building surrounded by greenery, drove a brand-new BMW sedan, and had an expensive stereo system in her living room. It was a high-end Accuphase pre-main amp and CD player, with large, smart-looking Linn speakers. And she always dressed in attractive, neat outfits.

I don't know that much about women's clothes, but even I could tell they were pricey, designer items.

When it came to music, she was eloquent. She had a sharp ear, and quickly chose the most precise way of describing what she'd heard. Her knowledge of music, too, was deep and broad. But when it came to anything other than music, she was pretty much an enigma. I tried my best to draw her out, but she would never open up.

One time she told me about Schumann.

"Like Schubert," she said, "Schumann battled VD when he was young, and the disease gradually affected his mind. Plus, he had schizophrenic tendencies. He regularly suffered from terrible auditory hallucinations, and his body was seized by uncontrollable trembling. He was convinced he was being pursued by evil spirits, and believed in their literal existence. Pursued by endless, horrific nightmares, he tried numerous times to kill himself. Once he even flung himself into the Rhine River. Inner delusions and outer reality were intertwined within him. **Carnaval** was an early work, so the evil spirits of his weren't showing their faces clearly yet. Since the piece is about the carnival festival, it's full of figures wearing cheerful-looking masks, but this was not merely some happy carnival. Ultimately the evil spirits lurking within him do make an appearance in the piece, one after the other, as if introduced for a moment, wearing happy carnival masks. All around them, an ominous early-spring wind is blowing. Meat, dripping with blood, is served to everyone. Carnival is literally the festival of thankfulness for meat, and a farewell to it, as Lent begins. That's exactly the kind of music it is."

"So the performer has to express,

musically, both the mask and the face that lies beneath it for all the characters who appear. Is that what you're saying?" I asked.

She nodded. "That's right. That's exactly right. If you can't express that sentiment, then what's the point in performing it? The piece is the ideal of playful music, but within that playfulness, you can catch a glimpse of the specters lurking inside the psyche. The playful sounds lure them out from the darkness."

She was silent for a while, and then continued.

"All of us, more or less, wear masks. Because without masks we can't survive in this violent world. Beneath an evil-spirit mask lies the natural face of an angel, beneath an angel's mask lies the face of an evil spirit. It's impossible to have just one or the other. That's who we are. And that's **Carnaval**. Schumann was able to see the many faces of humanity—the masks and the real faces—because he himself was a deeply divided soul, a person who lived in the stifling gap in between the two."

PERHAPS what she really wanted to say was **an ugly mask and a beautiful face beneath it—a beautiful mask and an ugly face**. This thought struck me at the time. Maybe she was really talking about some aspect of herself.

"For some people, the mask might become so tightly stuck that they can't remove it," I said.

"Yes," she said quietly. "Maybe that's true." She gave a faint smile. "But even if a mask gets stuck and can't be removed, that doesn't change the fact that beneath it, the real face remains."

"Though no one can ever see it."

She shook her head. "There must be

people who can. Surely there must be, somewhere."

"But Robert Schumann could see them. And he was unhappy. Because of the syphilis, schizophrenia, and evil spirits."

"He did leave behind this wonderful music, though," she said. "The kind of amazing music that no one else could write." She cracked each knuckle of both hands, loudly, in turn. "Because of the syphilis, schizophrenia, and evil spirits. Happiness is always a relative thing. Don't you think?"

"Could be," I said.

"Vladimir Horowitz once recorded Schumann's F Minor Sonata for the radio," she said. "Have you heard this story?"

"No, I don't think so," I replied. Listening to (and, I imagine) playing Schumann's Piano Sonata no. 3 must be a laborious task.

"When he listened to this recording on the radio later, Horowitz sat there, his head in his hands, totally depressed. He said it was awful."

She swirled the red wine around in her half-full glass and stared at it for a while.

"And this is what he said: 'Schumann was crazy, but I ruined him.' Don't you love that?"

"I do," I agreed.

I FOUND HER, in a way, an attractive woman, though I never really thought about her sexually. In that sense, my wife's judgment was correct. But it wasn't her unattractiveness that kept me from having sex with her. I don't think her ugliness by itself would have prevented us from sleeping together. What kept me from making love with her—from actually ever feeling that I wanted to—wasn't so much the beauty or ugliness of her mask, but more my fear of what I'd see lying beneath. Whether it was the face of evil, or the face of an angel.

IN OCTOBER F* stopped getting in touch with me. I'd gotten two new, rather intriguing CDs of **Carnaval**, and called her a few times, thinking we could listen to them together, but her cell phone always went to voice mail. I emailed her a few times, but got no response. A few autumn weeks passed, and October was over. November came, and people started wearing coats. This was the longest we'd gone without being in touch. I figured maybe she was on a long trip, or maybe wasn't feeling well.

It was my wife who first spotted her on TV. I was at my desk in my room, working.

"I could be wrong, but I think your girlfriend's on the TV news," my wife said. Come to think of it, she'd never once used F*'s name. It was always "your girlfriend." But by the time I got to the TV, the news had already switched to a report on a baby panda.

I waited until noon and watched the next news program then. F* appeared on the fourth news item. She was shown emerging from what looked like a police precinct, walking down the stairs, and getting into a black van. That slow journey was caught entirely on camera. No doubt about it, there was F*. There was no mistaking her face. It looked like she was handcuffed, for she had both hands in front of her, covered by a dark-colored coat. Female officers stood on either side of her, holding her arms. But she held her head high. Her lips were closed, and her gaze was calm as she looked straight ahead. Her eyes, however, were completely expressionless, like fish eyes. Other than a few strands of loose hair, she looked the same as usual. Still, her face on TV lacked that certain **something** that always gave it a lively quality. Or perhaps she was intentionally concealing it beneath a mask.

The woman announcer gave F*'s real name and detailed how the precinct had arrested her as an accomplice in a large-scale fraud. According to the report, the principal offender was her husband, who'd been arrested a few days before. They played a video of when he'd been taken into custody. This was the first time I'd ever seen her husband, and frankly I was struck speechless by how handsome he was. He was a gorgeous man, almost unreal in his attractiveness, like a professional model. He was said to be six years younger than her.

There wasn't any reason, of course, for me to be shocked by the fact that she'd married a handsome man six years her junior. There are all kinds of ill-matched couples. I know a few myself. Still, when I tried to picture the details of their daily life—F* and this staggeringly attractive man, living under one roof in that tidy condo in Daikanyama—I couldn't help but feel bewildered. I imagine most people seeing them on the news might be surprised by their pairing, but the sense of discomfort I felt then was far more individual, like an actual tingling pain on my skin. There was something unhealthy about it, like the feeling of helpless impotence you get when you've been taken in by a bizarre scheme.

The crime they were accused of was asset management fraud. They'd created a bogus investment company, solicited funds from ordinary people, promising a high rate of return, but actually didn't do any asset management whatsoever, simply shifting funds back and forth to offset shortfalls in any which way. It was obviously a scheme that would collapse. Why would such an intelligent woman, someone with such a deep appreciation of Schumann's piano music, assist in such a senseless crime, something she'd always be stuck with? The whole thing was beyond me. Maybe some negative force in her relationship with that man had sucked her into some criminal vortex. Maybe her own evil spirit was quietly hidden at its center. That's the only way I could fathom it.

All told, they were responsible for more than $10 million in losses. Most of the victims were elderly pensioners. A few of them were interviewed on TV, and I learned that every penny of their precious retirement savings, all they had to live on, had been snatched away. I felt sorry for them, but it was done. The whole thing was a mediocre crime. For some reason lots of people seem drawn in by such banal lies. Maybe it's the very mediocrity that attracts them, who knows? The world is swarming with hustlers, and with gullible people too. No matter how it was presented on TV, no matter who was at fault, this was a clear-cut fact, like the ebb and flow of the tide.

"So what are you going to do?" my wife asked me after the news was over.

"What do you mean? What **can** I do?" I said, switching off the TV with the remote.

"But she's your friend, isn't she?"

"We just get together once in a while and talk about music. I know nothing other than that."

"She never suggested you invest with them?"

Silently, I shook my head. For what it's worth, she never tried to get me involved in that sort of thing. That much I can say for sure.

"I didn't know her well, but I never thought she was someone who'd do something terrible like that," my wife said. "I guess you never can tell."

No, I suddenly thought, that's not exactly true. F* had a kind of special aura about her that drew people in. And within that—inside those peculiar, unusual features of hers—existed a kind of power that encroached on others' minds and hearts. It aroused my curiosity about her. And when that special attractive force merged with her young husband's spectacular looks, anything became possible and, perhaps, irresistible. An evil dynamic arose out of this, one that exceeded any common sense or logic.

Though I had no way of ever knowing what had brought this unlikeliest of pairs together.

For several days the TV news covered the incident, endlessly replaying the same clips. Her dead-fish eyes staring straight ahead, her handsome younger husband confronting the banks of cameras. The corners of his thin lips were, perhaps instinctively, raised slightly. The kind of smile that professional movie stars have when they need it. It looked like he was sending out a smile to the whole world. There was something about his face that resembled a well-constructed mask. At any rate, a week later, the arrests were all but forgotten. At least, the TV stations were no longer interested. I continued to follow the story in newspapers and weekly magazines, but eventually these stories tapered off too, like a stream of water being sucked into the sand. Finally, they came to an end altogether.

And then F* completely disappeared from my world. I had no clue where she was. There was no way of knowing if she was still in detention, or in jail, or was at home out on bail. There weren't any articles about her being on trial, though there must have been one, for the fraud was large enough to warrant some sort of sentence. At least according to the newspaper and magazine articles I'd read, it was crystal clear that she'd actively helped her husband in breaking the law.

A LONG TIME has passed since then, and still, whenever there's a concert featuring a performance of Schumann's **Carnaval**, I try to attend. And I scan the entire hall, and the lobby when I'm enjoying a glass of wine at intermission, looking for her. I've never found her, but I always feel that at any moment, she'll appear in the midst of the crowd.

I've kept on buying any new CDs of **Carnaval**. And I still rank them in my notebook. A lot of new recordings have appeared, yet my number one favorite is still the one by Rubinstein. Rubinstein's piano doesn't rip off people's masks. Instead, his playing gently, lightly, wafts through the interstice between the mask and the reality.

Happiness is always a relative thing. Don't you think?

THIS IS SOMETHING that happened long before any of this.

Back when I was in college, I once had a date with a girl who was fairly unattractive.

Actually, scratch the "fairly" part. It was a double date that a friend of mine set up, and she was the one who showed up as my date. She and my friend's girlfriend were in the same college dorm, and they were a year behind me in school. We had a quick meal together, the four of us, then we paired off and went our own way. It was the end of autumn.

She and I strolled around a park, then went into a café and talked over some coffee. She was short, with small eyes, and seemed like a nice person. She spoke in a quietly shy, distinct voice. She must have had excellent vocal cords. I'm in the tennis club in college, she told me. Her parents loved tennis, she added, and she'd played it with them since she was little. A healthy family, by the sound of it. And a family that probably got along well, too. But I'd hardly ever played tennis, so that put a damper on that subject. I loved jazz, but she knew next to nothing about it. So it was hard to find any subjects to talk about. Still, she said she'd like to hear more about jazz, so I launched into a monologue on Miles Davis and Art Pepper, and how I got interested in jazz, what drew me to it. She listened attentively, but I'm not sure how much she really got. Then I walked her to the train station and we said goodbye.

As we said goodbye she gave me the phone number to her dorm. She wrote the number down on a blank page in her notebook, neatly tore it out, and handed it to me. But I never called her.

A few days later I ran across my friend who'd invited me on the double date, and he apologized.

"I'm sorry for hooking you up with that—how should I put it?—unattractive girl the other day," he said. "I was planning on introducing you to someone really cute, but at the last minute something came up and she had to bail, so we asked the other girl to fill in. There was no one else in the dorm at the time. My girlfriend wanted to tell you she's sorry, too. I'll make it up to you. I promise."

After my friend said this, I felt like I should call the girl. Certainly she was no beauty, but she was more than just some "unattractive girl." There was a slight difference between the two, and I didn't want to leave it at that. I don't know how to put it, but it seemed important to me. I couldn't let it go. Most likely I'd never want her as my girlfriend. But I wouldn't mind seeing her and talking again. I didn't know what we'd talk about, but I was sure we'd find something. I couldn't just file her away under "Ugly Girl" and walk away.

But I couldn't find the paper with her number. I remembered putting it in my coat pocket, but it was nowhere to be found. I might have accidentally tossed it away with some receipt I didn't need. That's probably what happened. The upshot was, I couldn't phone her. If I'd asked my friend, he could have given me the dorm's number, but I wasn't wild about the idea of his reaction when I did, and I couldn't bring myself to ask.

I forgot that whole incident for a long time, and never tried to replay it in my mind. But here, as I write about F* and the way she looked, the whole thing has suddenly come back to me. In every detail.

In the end of autumn when I was twenty, I had a one-time-only date with a **not-so-attractive** girl, and we walked around a park as the day drew to an end.

As we had a cup of coffee I explained the finer points of Art Pepper's alto sax, how he'd make this amazing screeching sound with it sometimes. Which wasn't just some musical breakdown, I went on, but an important expression of his state of mind (yes, I actually did use that expression, believe it or not). And then I lost, forever, her phone number. **Forever**, needless to say, is a very long time.

THESE WERE BOTH nothing more than a pair of minor incidents that happened in my trivial little life. Short side trips along the way. Even if they hadn't happened, I doubt my life would have wound up much different from what it is now. But still, these memories return to me sometimes, traveling down a very long passageway to arrive. And when they do, their unexpected power shakes me to the core. Like an autumn wind that gusts at night, swirling fallen leaves in a forest, flattening the pampas grass in fields, and pounding hard on the doors to people's homes, over and over again.

THE YAKULT SWALLOWS

POETRY COLLECTION

'D LIKE TO MAKE THIS CLEAR from the start: I **love** baseball. And what I really love is actually going to a stadium and watching a live game played out right in front of me. I slap on my baseball cap and take along my glove in case I happen to catch a foul ball from the infield seats, or a home-run ball if I'm sitting in the outfield seats. Watching broadcasts of games on TV doesn't do it for me. I always get the feeling I'm missing something vital. Like with sex, when you . . . hold on, let's not go there. In any

272 FIRST PERSON SINGULAR

event, watching baseball on TV robs me of that heart-pounding excitement of a live game. At least that's how I feel. Though if I were asked to list the reasons why and explain them all, I doubt I could.

To be clear, I'm a fan of the Yakult Swallows. I wouldn't say I'm a wildly enthusiastic, devout fan, but I do consider myself a pretty loyal supporter. At least, I've cheered on the team for a long time. I've been frequenting Jingu Stadium from back when the team was called the Sankei Atoms. That's why I lived near the stadium. Actually, that still holds true. When it comes to finding places to live in Tokyo, that's my main condition—that the condo be within walking distance of Jingu Stadium. And, unsurprisingly, I also own several team jerseys and baseball caps.

.   .   .

JINGU STADIUM has long been a peaceful, humble ballpark, not the sort of stadium setting any attendance records. What I mean to say is that the place is almost always a bit deserted. Except for rare occasions, it's never been sold out and I can always get a ticket. By "rare occasions" I mean like when you're out for a walk at night and encounter a lunar eclipse, or run across a friendly male calico cat at the neighborhood park—I mean it's about as likely as those occurrences. But truthfully I kind of enjoy how sparsely populated it is. I've always disliked crowds, even as a child.

I don't mean to imply that the reason I became a Yakult Swallows fan is the half-deserted stadium. I'd feel sorry for the team if I said something like that. The poor Yakult Swallows. And poor Jingu Stadium. I mean, the section where the visiting team's fans sit always seems to fill up faster than the Yakult Swallows fans' section. You could search the entire world and I doubt you'd find another baseball stadium where that's the case.

So why did I become a fan of that team, anyway? What long and winding path led me to become a longtime supporter of the Swallows? What sort of galaxy did I cross to make that fleeting, dim star—the one that's the hardest to locate in the night sky—my own lucky star? It's kind of a long story, but under the circumstances maybe I should touch on it. Who knows, but it might end up being a kind of concise autobiography.

I WAS BORN IN KYOTO, but we soon moved to the Kansai-Kobe area, where I lived till I was eighteen, first in Shukugawa, and then in Ashiya. When I was free, I'd ride my bike, or sometimes take the Hanshin railway line, to see a game at Koshien Stadium, the home of the Hanshin Tigers. I was, as an elementary school student, naturally a member of the Hanshin Tigers Fan Club. (You got bullied at school if you weren't.) I don't care what anyone says, Koshien is the most beautiful stadium in all of Japan. Back when I was a boy, I'd rush to the stadium with my ticket in hand, pass through the ivy-covered entrance, and hurry up the dimly lit concrete stairs. And when the natural grass of the outfield leapt into view, and that brilliant ocean of green spread out before me, my little heart beat loudly with excitement, for all the world as if a group of lively dwarves were bungee-jumping inside my tiny ribs.

On the field, there is a story line about to be played out, amid the full array of cheers and signs and cries of anger ready and waiting: the players warming up, their uniforms still sparkling clean, the happy reverberation of the pure-white ball striking the sweet spot of the bat as the players field fungoes, the determined shouts of the hawkers selling beer, the fresh new scoreboard before the game begins. Yes, that's how—without any room for doubt whatsoever—that's how baseball, and going to the stadium, has become an integral part of me.

So at eighteen when I left the Kansai-Kobe area to go to college in Tokyo I decided, like it was the most natural thing, to go to Jingu Stadium and root for the Sankei Atoms. This was the closest stadium to where I was living, so I could root for the home team—which to me was the very best way of enjoying watching baseball. Though strictly speaking, Korakuen Stadium, the home of the Tokyo Giants back then, was a bit closer to my apartment . . . but there was no way I was going there. I mean, there are certain ethical standards you have to maintain.

This was in 1968. The Folk Crusaders had a big hit then with "I Only Live Twice," it was the year Martin Luther King and Robert Kennedy were assassinated, and there were student demonstrations on Anti-War Day that occupied Shinjuku station. Lining up all these events makes it sound like ancient history, but, at any rate, that was the year I decided, "Okay, I'm going to be a Sankei Atoms fan from now on." Prompted by something—fate, my astrological sign, blood type, prophecy, or a spell. If you have a chart of historical chronology I'd like you to write the following, in small letters in one corner: **1968. This was the year that Haruki Murakami became a Sankei Atoms fan.**

I'm ready to swear this before every god in the world, but at the time, the Sankei Atoms had totally hit rock bottom. They didn't have a single star player, the entire team was obviously barely scraping along, and there were hardly any fans at the stadium, except for when they played the Giants. To use an antiquated Japanese term, "the black cuckoo was calling"—meaning the place was deserted. The thought often struck me back then that the team mascot shouldn't be the anime character Astro Boy (Iron-arm Atom, in the original) but instead should be a black cuckoo. Though what exactly that kind of cuckoo looked like, I couldn't tell you.

This was the age when the Tokyo Giants—under their manager, Tetsuharu Kawakami—ruled. Their home ground, Korakuen Stadium, was always sold out. Their corporate owner, the Yomiuri

Shimbun newspaper group, used game tickets as a major sales strategy, and worked hard to increase newspaper sales. The Giants sluggers Sadaharu Oh and Shigeo Nagashima were national heroes. I passed by kids on the street who proudly wore their Giants baseball caps. But a kid wearing a Sankei Atoms cap was nowhere to be seen. Perhaps those brave few who did were seen stealthily slinking down back alleyways, furtively weaving their way under the eaves. My gosh—where is there any justice left in the world?

But whenever I had free time (and back then I was free most of the time), I'd walk over to Jingu Stadium and silently root for the Sankei Atoms by myself. They lost much more often than they won (probably losing about two-thirds of their games), but I was still young. As long as I could stretch out on the grass past the outfield, have some beers, and watch the game, occasionally gazing aimlessly up at the sky, I was pretty happy. I'd enjoy it when the team won the odd game, and when they lost, I'd console myself with the thought that **it's important in life to get used to losing**. They didn't have bleachers in the outfield then, just a slope with trampled-down grass. I'd spread out a newspaper (the **Sankei Sports** paper, of course) and sit there, sometimes lying back. As you can imagine, when it rained the ground got pretty muddy.

IN 1978, when the team won its first championship, I was living in Sendagaya, a ten-minute walk from the stadium, so I went to see games whenever I was free. That year the Yakult Swallows (they'd changed their name to the Yakult Swallows by then) won their first league championship in the twenty-nine-year history of the franchise, and rode that wave all the way to victory in the Japan Series. A miraculous year, for sure. That was the same year (when I was twenty-nine, too) that I wrote my first novel, entitled **Hear the Wind Sing**, which won the Gunzo Newcomer's Prize. I suppose that's when you could call me a novelist, starting then. I know it's just a coincidence, but I can't help feeling there's some connection, some karma, at work in all this.

But this was all much later. In the ten years that led up to that moment, from 1968 to 1977, I witnessed a huge number, an almost astronomical number (at least that's the way it feels), of losing games. To put it another way, I steadily became accustomed to regular loss: "Here we go again—another defeat." Like a diver carefully takes his time to acclimate to the different water pressure. It's true that life brings us far more defeats than victories. And real-life wisdom arises not so much from knowing how we might beat someone as from learning how to accept defeat with grace.

"You'll never understand this advantage we've been given!" I often used to shout at the Giants' cheering section. (Of course I never actually shouted it aloud.)

DURING THOSE LONG DARK YEARS, like passing through an endless tunnel, I sat in the outfield seats. To kill time while I watched the game, I scribbled down some poem-like jottings in a notebook. Poems on the topic of baseball. Unlike soccer, with baseball there can be a lot of down time between plays, so I could look away from the field, jot down my ideas on paper without missing any runs. Let's face it—baseball is a sport done at a leisurely pace. Most of these poems were written during tiresome, losing games when one pitcher after another was brought in to try to salvage the game. (Oh, man, how many times did I watch that kind of game?)

THE FIRST POEM in my collection was the following one. There are two versions of the poem—a short version and a long one—and this is the long version. I added a few things later on.

RIGHT FIELDER

On that May afternoon
You're holding down right field at
    Jingu Stadium.

The right fielder for the Sankei Atoms.
That's your profession.
I'm seated in the back of the right
     field's seats,
Drinking slightly lukewarm beer.
Like always.
The opposing team's batter lofts a fly to
     right field.
A simple pop fly.
It arcs high up, a lazy fly ball.
The wind has stopped.
And the sun isn't an issue.
It's a piece of cake.
You raise both hands a bit,
And step forward about three yards.
You got this.
I take a sip of beer,
Waiting for the ball to drop.
As straight as a ruler the ball falls
Precisely three yards behind you.
Like a mallet lightly tapping the edge
     of the universe,

There's a slight **plunk**.
It makes me wonder—
Why in the world do I cheer on a team
    like this?
This itself is a kind of—
Riddle as huge as the universe.

I have no idea if this could be called a poem. If you did, it might make actual poets upset, make them want to string me up from the nearest light pole. I'll pass on that, thank you very much. Okay, but then what **should** I call these? If there's a better name for them, then I'd like to know it. So, for the time being, at least, I labeled them "poems." And I gathered my poems into a book called **The Yakult Swallows Poetry Collection** and published it. If poets want to get all bent out of shape over it, then be my guest. This was in 1982. A little before I finished writing my novel **A Wild Sheep Chase**, three years after I'd debuted as a novelist (if you could call it that).

Major publishers were wise enough, of course, not to show even a smidge of interest in putting out my book of poems, so I ended up basically self-publishing it. Fortunately a friend of mine ran a printing company, so I could print it up on the cheap. Simple binding, five hundred numbered copies, each and every one signed by yours truly. Haruki Murakami, Haruki Murakami, Haruki Murakami . . . Predictably, though, hardly anyone paid it any attention. You'd have to have pretty odd taste to lay down good money for something like that. I think I sold about three hundred copies, all told. The rest I gave away as souvenirs to various friends and acquaintances. Nowadays they've become valuable collector's items, and fetch unbelievable prices. You never know what's going to happen. I only have two copies myself. If only I'd kept more, I'd be rolling in dough by now.

．

AFTER MY FATHER'S FUNERAL, three of my cousins and I drank a ton of beer. Two of my cousins were on my father's side (around the same age as me), and the third was a cousin on my mother's side (about fifteen years younger). We sat around till late at night, throwing back the beers. Beer was all we drank. And no snacks, either. Just an endless parade of beer. I'd never drunk that much beer in my life. By the end, about twenty of those large, twenty-one-ounce Kirin bottles stood empty on the table. How my bladder held out, I have no idea. On top of that, while we were downing all this beer, I stepped out to a jazz bar near the funeral home and had several Four Roses whiskeys on the rocks.

I don't know why I drank so much that night. It wasn't like I felt any deep emotions or anything—I wasn't feeling particularly sad or empty. No matter how much I drank, though, I didn't get drunk, and the next day, I didn't even have a speck of a hangover. In fact, when I woke up the next morning, my mind was sharper than usual.

My father was a dyed-in-the-wool Hanshin Tigers fan. When I was a kid, my father was in a foul mood whenever the Tigers lost. Even his facial expression would change. And if he had anything to drink, this tendency would get even worse. So on nights after the Hanshin Tigers lost, I'd be extra careful not to do anything to upset him. Possibly that's why I never got to be—or never **could** be—a Hanshin Tigers fan.

My relationship with my father wasn't what you'd call friendly. There were lots of reasons for this, but in the twenty years before severe diabetes and the cancer that had spread throughout his body put an end to his life at age ninety, my father and I hardly exchanged a word with each other. You could never label that a "friendly relationship." At the very end of his life, we had a reconciliation of sorts, though perhaps it came too late to really matter.

But of course I do have some wonderful memories.

When I was nine, in the fall, the St. Louis Cardinals played a goodwill game against an All-Star Japanese team. The great Stan Musial was at his peak then, and he faced two top Japanese pitchers, Kazuhisa Inao and Tadashi Sugiura, in an amazing showdown. My father and I went to Koshien Stadium to see the game. We were in the infield seats along first base, near the front. Before the game began, the Cardinals' players made a circuit of the whole stadium, tossing signed soft rubber tennis balls to the crowd. People leapt to their feet, shouting, vying to grab the balls. But I just sat in my seat, vacantly watching all of this happen. I figured that a little kid like me had no chance of getting one of those signed balls. The next instant, however, I suddenly found one of them in my lap. By total chance, it just happened to land there. **Plop**—like some divine revelation.

"Good for you," my father told me. He sounded half shocked, half admiring. Come to think of it, when I became a novelist at age thirty, he said almost the same thing to me. Half shock, half admiration.

That was probably the greatest, most

memorable thing that happened to me when I was a boy. Maybe the most blessed event I ever experienced. Could it be that my love for baseball stadiums sprang from this incident? I took that treasured white ball back home, of course, but that's all I remember about it. What ever happened to that ball? Where could it have possibly gone?

.

I ALSO INCLUDED the following poem in **The Yakult Swallows Poetry Collection.** I believe I wrote it back when Osamu Mihara had taken charge of the team as their manager. This was the period I have the most vivid and fond memories of, for whatever reason. I was always fired up to go to the stadium back then, sure that something fun and unexpected was going to happen.

A BIRD'S SHADOW

An afternoon day game in early
   summer.
Top of the eighth
The Swallows losing 9–1 (or
   something like that).
Their sixth pitcher (or something
   like that), someone I'd never
   heard of,
Was warming up.
Right at the instant
The clear-cut shadow of a bird
Raced quickly from first base
Over the green grass to where the
   center fielder stood.
I looked up at the sky
But couldn't spot the bird.
The sun was too bright.
All I saw was a shadow, like a black
   cutout, falling on the grass.

A bird-shaped shadow.
Was this some lucky omen?
Or an unlucky one?
I gave it some serious thought,
But soon shook my head.
Come on, knock it off.
How could there ever be a lucky omen
  at a place like **this**?

.

WHEN MY MOTHER'S MEMORY started to get shaky, and she couldn't live on her own anymore, I went back to her house in Kansai to get her ready to move out. I couldn't believe all of the junk—at least, that's how it seemed to me—that she had stored away in boxes. She'd bought an unimaginable amount of stuff for reasons I couldn't fathom.

For instance, one empty candy box was stuffed full of cards. Mostly telephone cards, the kind people once used for pay phones, with a few prepaid railway cards for the Hanshin or Hankyu Railways mixed in. All the cards had Tigers players' photos on them—Kanemoto, Imaoka, Yano, Akahoshi, Fujikawa . . . Telephone cards? Good grief. Where the heck are you supposed to use telephone cards these days?

I didn't count them all, but there must have been over a hundred. I just couldn't get it. As far as I knew, my mother had no interest in baseball whatsoever. Yet it was clear that she was the one who'd bought all those cards. There was solid proof. Had she become a rabid Hanshin Tigers fan before I realized it? For all that, she flatly denied ever buying so many Hanshin Tigers telephone cards. "What are you talking about?" she said. "I'd never buy those kinds of things. Ask your father—he'll know."

So what was I supposed to do? My father had died three years before this.

The upshot is that, although I have a cell phone, I've been walking all over, looking hard for the rare public phone, trying to use up these Hanshin Tigers telephone cards. Thanks to this, I've gotten to know their players' names pretty well, though most of the ones on the cards have either retired by now or have moved on to other teams.

The Hanshin Tigers.

The Tigers used to have a player named Mike Reinbach, an outfielder, a high-spirited, all-around nice guy. I wrote one poem in which he was featured in a supporting role. Reinbach was the same age as me. He was killed in a car accident in the U.S. in 1989. In 1989 I was living in Rome, writing a long novel. So I didn't learn of his death, at age thirty-nine, for quite some time. Italian newspapers, as you can imagine, weren't going to report on the death of a former Hanshin Tigers outfielder.

This is the poem I wrote.

OUTFIELDERS' BUTTS

I enjoy gazing at the butts of
   outfielders.
What I mean is, when I'm watching a
   slow-going, losing game
From the outfield seats by myself,
How else can I enjoy myself besides
   staring at the outfielders' butts?
If there's some other way, I'd sure like
   to know.
I could talk the night away
About outfielders' glutes.
The Swallows' center fielder John
   Scott's* butt

---

* John Scott played outfield for the Swallows from 1979 to 1981. He once hit four home runs in a double

Is beautiful beyond measure.
His legs are ridiculously long
And look as if they're suspended in
    the air.
Like a bold metaphor that makes your
    heart sing.
Compared to this, the legs of the left
    fielder, Wakamatsu,
Are incredibly short.
When the two players stand together
Scott's butt is about at the level of
    Wakamatsu's chin.
The Tigers' Reinbach* has a butt
So symmetrical you can't help but
    love it.
Just one look and it all makes sense.

---

header. Twice he won the Diamond Glove Award, Japan's equivalent of the Gold Glove.

* Mike Reinbach played outfield for the Hanshin Tigers from 1976 to 1980. Along with Hal Breeden he was one of their cleanup hitters. He was a gutsy player who was very popular with fans.

The butt of the Hiroshima Carp's
    player Shane[*]
Is deeply thoughtful, cerebral.
Reflective, you might say.
People really should have called him by
    his full name,
Scheinblum.
If for nothing else, then to show
    respect for that one-of-a-kind butt.
I was about to list
The names of outfielders whose
    butts
Are not what you'd call attractive—
But decided I'd better not.
After all, you have to consider their
    mothers and siblings, and wives
And kids, if they have any.

---

[*] Richard Alan Scheinblum played outfield for the Hiroshima Carp from 1975 to 1976. He also played in an All Star game in the Major Leagues. His name was shortened to "Shane" in Japan. "I don't mind," he commented. "Though I can't ride a horse."

AS A YAKULT FAN I did once watch a Hanshin Tigers vs. Swallows game at Koshien Stadium, the Tigers' home stadium. I happened to have an errand that brought me to Kobe and I had the afternoon free. I saw a poster at the Hanshin Sannomiya station advertising a day game at Koshien Stadium and decided it'd been far too long since my last visit to Koshien. It had been over thirty years, in fact.

Katsuya Nomura was the Swallows' manager back then. This was when players like Furuta, Ikeyama, Miyamoto, and Inaba were at their peak (a happy time for the team, now that I think of it). So, naturally, the following poem wasn't included in the original **Yakult Swallows Poetry Collection**. I wrote it long after that collection was published.

I didn't have a pen or any paper on me

that day, so as soon as I got back to the hotel, I used the stationery in the room to scribble down this (sort of) poem. A memo that just happened to take the form of a poem, I suppose you could call it. My desk drawer is full of memos and fragments of writing like that. They don't actually serve much purpose, but I keep them nonetheless.

AN ISLAND IN THE OCEAN
CURRENT

That summer afternoon
I searched for the Yakult Swallows fans'
    section
In the left-field bleachers at Koshien
    Stadium.
It took a long time to find it,
Since the section for the Yakult fans
    was a tiny area
only five yards square.

All around, on every side, were crowds
   of Tigers fans.
It reminded me of the John Ford
   movie **Fort Apache**.
The small troop of cavalry led by the
   obstinate Henry Fonda
Were surrounded by a huge mass of
   Indians that blanketed the ground.
The cavalry was cornered, backs to the
   wall.
Like a small island in an ocean
   current
They bravely raised a single flag in their
   midst.

Now that I think of it, when I was in
   elementary school
I sat in these very seats, watching
   Sadaharu Oh, a high schooler then,
   play.
This was the spring national high
   school baseball tournament

When his school, Waseda Jitsugyo
    High School, won.
He was their star, batting fourth.
The memory of that day is so very clear
    in my mind,
As if watching it from a backward
    telescope.
So far away, yet so very close.
And right now I am surrounded by
    fierce Indians in pinstripes,
And under the Yakult Swallows' flag I
    raise my plaintive cheer.
I've been away from my hometown for
    such a long time, and
My heart aches here
On this tiny, solitary island in the
    ocean current.

.

AT ANY RATE, of all the baseball stadiums in the world, I like being in Jingu
Stadium the best of all. In an infield

seat behind first base, or in the right-field bleachers. I love all the sounds, the smells, the way I can sit there, just gazing up at the sky. I love the breeze caressing my skin, I love sipping an ice-cold beer, observing the people around me. Whether the team wins or loses, I love the time spent there most of all.

Of course, winning is much better than losing. No argument there. But winning or losing doesn't affect the weight and value of the time. It's the same time, either way. A minute is a minute, an hour is an hour. We need to cherish it. We need to deftly reconcile ourselves with time, and leave behind as many precious memories as we can—that's what's the most valuable.

The first thing I like to do when I take my seat at the stadium is have a dark beer—a stout. But there aren't many vendors selling dark beer at the stadium.

It takes time to locate one. When I finally locate one, I raise my hand and call out. The vendor makes his way over. A skinny young guy, undernourished looking. He has longish hair. Probably a high school student doing this as a part-time job. He comes over, and the first thing he does is apologize. "I'm sorry, but all I have is dark beer," he says.

"No need to apologize," I say, reassuring him. "I mean, I've been waiting a long time for someone selling dark beer to come by."

"Thank you," he says. And cracks a cheerful smile.

I imagine this young vendor will have to apologize to lots of people this evening. "I'm sorry, but all I have is dark beer," since most people at the stadium probably wanted regular lager. I pay him for the beer and leave him with a small word of encouragement: "Good luck to you!"

When I write novels, I often experience the same feeling as that young man. I want to face people in the world and apologize to each and every one. **"I'm sorry, but all I have is dark beer."**

But no matter. Let's not get into novels here. Tonight's game is about to begin. I'm praying that our team wins. But at the same time quietly steeling myself for the possibility of yet another loss.

FIRST PERSON

SINGULAR

I HARDLY EVER WEAR SUITS. At most, maybe two or three times a year, since there are rarely any situations where I need to get dressed up. I may wear a casual jacket on occasion, but no tie, or leather shoes. That's the type of life I chose for myself, so that's how things have worked out.

Sometimes, though, even when there's no need for it, I do decide to wear a suit and tie. Why? When I open my closet and check out what kind of clothes are there (I have to do that or else I don't know what kind of clothes I own), and gaze at the suits I've hardly ever worn, the dress shirts still in the dry cleaner's plastic garment bags, and the ties that look brand new, no trace of ever having been used, I start to feel apologetic toward these clothes. Then I try them on just to see how they look. I experiment with various tie knots to see if I still remember how to do them. Including one making a proper dimple. The only time I do all this is when I'm home alone. If someone else is here, I'd have to explain what I'm up to.

Once I go to the trouble of getting the outfit on, it seems a waste to take it all off right away, so I go out for a while dressed up like that. Strolling around town in a suit and tie. And it feels pretty good. I get the sense that even my facial expression and gait are transformed. It's an invigorating sensation, as if I've temporarily stepped away from the everyday. But after an hour or so of roaming, this newness fades. I get tired of wearing a suit and tie, the tie starts to feel itchy and too tight, like it's choking me. The leather shoes click too hard and loud as they strike the pavement. So I go home, slip off the leather shoes, peel off the suit and tie, change into a worn-out set of sweatpants and sweatshirt, plop down on the sofa, and feel relaxed and at peace. This is my little one-hour secret ceremony, entirely harmless—or at least not something I need to feel guilty about.

I WAS ALONE in the house that day. My wife had gone out to eat Chinese food. I never eat Chinese food (I think I'm allergic to some of the spices they use), so she goes with a close girlfriend of hers whenever she has a craving.

After a quick dinner, I put on an old

Joni Mitchell album and settled down in my special reading chair and read a mystery. I loved this album, and the novel was the very latest by one of my favorite authors. But for some reason I couldn't settle down, couldn't focus on either the music or the book. I considered watching a movie I'd recorded, but couldn't find one I really wanted to see. Some days are like that. You have time on your hands, and you try to decide what you want to do, but can't come up with a thing. There should have been tons of things I wanted to do . . . As I wandered aimlessly around the room an idea struck me: I haven't tried on a suit in ages, so why not?

I laid out a Paul Smith suit on the bed (one I'd bought out of necessity but had only worn twice), and picked out a tie and shirt that would go well with it. A light gray, widespread-collar shirt and an Ermenegildo Zegna tie with an elaborate paisley pattern that I'd bought at the Rome airport. I stood in front of the full-length mirror and checked how I looked. Not bad, I concluded. At least nothing was obviously wrong with the outfit.

But on that particular day as I stood in front of the mirror, an uncomfortable feeling came over me, a twinge of remorse. Remorse? How should I put it? . . . I imagine it was like the guilty conscience someone feels who goes through life having embellished a resumé. It might not be illegal, but it's a misrepresentation that raises a lot of ethical issues. You know it's wrong, you know nothing good will come of it, yet you can't help yourself. There's a certain kind of uneasiness that those kinds of actions engender. I'm just imagining this, but it might be similar to the feeling of men who secretly dress up as women.

But it's weird that I should feel this

way. I've been an upstanding adult for years now, I pay what I owe for my taxes on time, I've never broken the law, other than a few traffic tickets, and I might not be the most cultured person around, but I'm refined enough. I even know who was older—Bartók or Stravinsky. (I doubt few other people do.) And these clothes I had on were items I'd paid for with income acquired by working every day, legally. Or at least not illegally. There was nothing anyone could blame me for. Okay—then why this guilty conscience? Why this edgy feeling that, ethically, something was amiss?

Well, everyone has days like that, I told myself. I would think even Django Reinhardt had nights when he flubbed a chord or two, and Niki Lauda some afternoons when he messed up changing gears. So I decided not to think any more deeply about it. Decked out in the suit

and tie, I slipped on a pair of leather cor-
dovan shoes and went out. I should have
followed my gut and stayed at home and
watched movies, but that was something
I only realized after the fact.

IT WAS A PLEASANT SPRING EVENING.
A bright, full moon hung in the sky, and
there were young green buds just appearing on the trees lining the streets. Perfect
weather for a walk. I strolled around for
a while, then decided to stop in a bar and
have a cocktail. Not the neighborhood
bar I frequented, but one a little farther
away that I'd never been to before. If I
went to my usual bar, I could count on
the bartender asking me, "Why the suit
and necktie today? Pretty unusual getup
for you, isn't it?" It was too much trouble
to explain the reason. I mean, to begin
with, there **wasn't** any reason.

It was still early evening, and I went downstairs to a basement-level bar. The only customers were two men in their forties seated across from each other at a table. Company employees on their way home from work, by the look of it, in dark suits and forgettable ties. The two of them were leaning forward, heads close together, discussing something in low voices. There was a pile of what looked like documents of some sort on the table. Must have been going over business, I figured. Or else predicting horse race results. Either way, nothing to do with me. I sat down away from them at the bar counter, choosing the stool with the best lighting, since I was planning to read, and ordered a vodka gimlet from the bow-tied, middle-aged bartender.

In a little while, a chilled drink was served on a paper coaster in front of me, and I pulled out the mystery novel from my pocket and continued reading. I had about a third of the way to go to the end. As I said, it was by a writer I'm pretty fond of, but sadly the plot of this newest book just didn't do it for me. On top of which, halfway through, I lost track of how the characters were related to each other. But I read on nonetheless, partly out of duty, partly out of habit. I've never liked giving up on a book once I've started it. I always hold out hope that there will be some riveting development toward the end, though the chances of that are pretty slim.

I slowly sipped my vodka gimlet and forged ahead another twenty pages in the book. For some reason, though, I still couldn't concentrate. And it wasn't simply because the novel wasn't the most riveting. It wasn't like the bar was noisy. (The background music was subdued, the lighting fine, almost the perfect atmosphere for enjoying a book.) I think it was due to that vague sense of unease I'd been feeling, that something just wasn't quite right, was slightly out of joint. Like the contents didn't fit the container, like the integrity of it all had been lost. I get that feeling from time to time.

In back of the bar was a shelf with an impressive lineup of bottles. And behind that was a large mirror, in which I was reflected. I stared at it for a while, and as you might expect, the me in the mirror stared back. A sudden thought hit me, that somewhere I'd taken a wrong turn in life. And the longer I stared at my image decked out in a suit and tie, this sensation only intensified. The more I stared at my image, the more it seemed less like me and more like someone I'd never seen before. But if this isn't me in the mirror, I thought, then who is it?

As is true of most people, I imagine, I had experienced a number of turning points in my life, where I could go either left or right. And each time I chose one, right or left. (There were times when there was a clear-cut reason, but most of the time there wasn't. And it wasn't always like I was making a choice, but more like **the choice itself** chose **me**.) And now here I was, a first person singular. If I'd chosen a different direction, most likely I wouldn't be here. But still—who **is** that in the mirror?

I CLOSED MY BOOK for a moment, looked away from the mirror, and took a couple of deep breaths.

The bar was starting to fill up. A woman was seated on my right, two empty stools away. She was drinking a pale green cocktail, but I didn't have a clue what it was called. She seemed to be alone, or maybe she was waiting for a friend to show up. I pretended to read and checked her out in the mirror. She wasn't young, probably fifty or so. She didn't seem to be making an effort to look younger than her age. She seemed pretty self-confident. She was petite, and slim, her hair cut just the right length. Her clothes were pretty chic—a striped dress in a soft-looking material, and a beige cashmere cardigan. She didn't have particularly beautiful features, but there was a kind of overall elegance to her. When she was a young woman, she must have been striking. Men must have always been flirting with her. I could sense memories of those days by the the way she held herself.

I called the bartender over, ordered a second vodka gimlet, munched on a few cashews, and went back to reading. Occasionally I touched the knot of my tie. Checking to make sure it was still neatly tied.

About fifteen minutes later, she was seated on the stool beside me. The bar was getting crowded, and she'd slid over to accommodate some newly arrived customers. I was sure now that she was alone. Under the recessed lighting, I read on until I had only a few pages left. The story still showed no signs of picking up.

"Excuse me," the woman suddenly said.

I raised my head and looked at her.

"You seem so into your book, but I wonder if you'd mind me asking you a question?" For such a petite woman, she had a low, deep voice. Not a cold voice, but certainly not one that sounded friendly, or inviting.

"Of course. This book isn't exactly spellbinding or anything," I said. I placed a bookmark inside the novel and shut it.

"What's so enjoyable about doing things like that?" she asked.

I couldn't understand what she was getting at. I twisted around to face her directly. I couldn't recall ever seeing her before. I'm not that great at remembering faces, but I was fairly certain we'd never met. I'd remember meeting her, for sure, if I had. She was that kind of woman.

"Things like that?" I repeated.

"All dressed up, alone at a bar, drinking a gimlet, quietly into your reading."

Like before, I still had no idea what she was trying to tell me. Though I could sense a kind of malice, an enmity in her tone. I gazed at her, waiting for her to go on. Her face was oddly expressionless. It was like she was determined to conceal any emotion on her face. She was silent for a long time. About a minute, I'd say.

"A vodka gimlet," I said to break the silence.

"What did you say?"

"It's not a gimlet, but a vodka gimlet." A pointless remark, perhaps, but there was a difference.

She gave a small, compact shake of her head, as if flitting away a tiny fly buzzing around her.

"Whatever. But do you think that's all pretty fantastic? Urbane, stylish, and smart and all?"

I probably should have paid my bill and left as soon as I could. That was the best reaction in a situation like this. The woman, for some reason, was picking a fight. Challenging me. What compelled her to do that, I had no idea. She might have just been in a foul mood. Or else something about me struck her the wrong way, jangled her nerves, irritated her. The chance of anything good coming from an encounter with someone like that was next to zero. The wise choice would have been to politely excuse myself, smile and stand up (the smile was optional), quickly pay my bill, and get as far away as I could. And I couldn't think of any reason not to. I'm not the type who can't stand to lose, and I don't like to fight when I can't see the justice in it. I'm more into silent, strategic withdrawals.

But for whatever reason, that's not what I did. **Something** stopped me. Curiosity, perhaps.

"Pardon me, but are we acquainted?" I ventured.

She narrowed her eyes and stared at me strangely. The frown lines next to her eyes deepened. "Acquainted?" she said, picked up her cocktail glass (this was her third drink, if memory serves), and took a sip of whatever it was inside—what, I had no idea. "**Acquainted**? How did you come up with **that** word?"

I searched my memory once more. Had I met this woman somewhere? The answer was—no. Clearly this was the first time I'd ever laid eyes on her.

"I'm thinking you must be mistaking me for someone else," I said. My voice was strangely flat, expressionless. It didn't even sound like me.

She smiled faintly, coldly. "Is that what you're going with?" she said, and set the thin Baccarat cocktail glass back down on the coaster in front of her.

"That's a lovely suit," she said. "Though it doesn't look good on you. It's like you're wearing borrowed clothes. And that tie—it doesn't exactly go with that suit. It's a little off. The tie is Italian, but the suit, I would say, is British made."

"You certainly know a lot about clothes."

"Know a lot about clothes?" She sounded a little taken aback. Her lips parted a fraction, and she gave me a hard stare. "Do you really need to say that? That goes without saying."

Goes without saying?

I searched my mind for the people I knew in the apparel industry. I only knew a handful, and all were men. None of this made any sense.

Why would this **go without saying?**

It crossed my mind to explain to her why I was wearing a suit and tie this evening, but I thought better of it. Explaining it wouldn't blunt the attack mode she was obviously in. It might, in fact, have the opposite effect, and only pour oil on what seemed to be angry flames.

I drank the last drops of my vodka gimlet and quietly got down off the bar stool. This seemed like my chance to put an end to the conversation.

"I think you're probably not **acquainted** with me," she said. I nodded. She was right.

"Not directly," she went on. "Though we did meet once. We didn't talk much then, so I think you're not really **acquainted** with me. And you were so very busy with other things then. As usual."

As usual?

"I'm a friend of a friend of yours," she said in a quietly firm tone. "This close friend of yours—this person who **used** to be your close friend, I should say—is quite upset with you, and I am just as upset with you as she is. You must know what I'm talking about. Think about it. About what happened three years ago, at the shore. About what a horrible, awful thing you did. You should be ashamed of yourself."

I'd had enough. I scooped up my book, only a few pages still unread, and stuck it in my jacket pocket. I'd long since lost any thought of finishing it.

I QUICKLY PAID MY BILL, in cash, and exited the bar. She didn't say anything more, just followed me fixedly with her eyes as I left. I never once turned around, yet I felt her intense gaze on my back until I made it outside. That sensation, like being jabbed with a long sharp needle, penetrated the fine cloth of my Paul Smith suit to make a deep, lasting mark on my back.

As I climbed the narrow staircase to ground level, I tried to gather my thoughts.

How should I have responded? Should I have asked her, "What in the world are you talking about?" and demanded that she explain herself? What she'd said struck me as totally unfair, something I had no memory of whatsoever.

But somehow, I couldn't. Why not? I think I was afraid. Afraid of learning that another me who wasn't really **me** had, at a **shore somewhere** three years before, committed a horrendous offense toward a woman, someone I probably didn't know. Afraid of having her drag out, into the light, something inside me, something completely unknown to me. Rather than face this, I chose to silently get up off my stool and make my getaway, all the while submitting to a torrent of what I could only see as groundless accusations.

Did I do the right thing? If the same thing happened to me again, would I act the same?

But this **shore** she mentioned—where could it be? The word had a strange ring to it. Was it by the ocean? A lake? A river? Or some other, peculiar assemblage of water? Three years ago was I next to some sizable body of water? I couldn't recall. I couldn't even grasp **when** three years ago had occurred. Everything she said sounded so specific, but at the same time symbolic. The parts were clear, yet the whole wasn't in focus. And that very discrepancy unsettled my nerves.

At any rate, the whole thing left a bad taste in my mouth. I tried to swallow it down but couldn't, tried to spit out but was unable to. I wanted to get angry, plain and simple. There was no reason I had to endure that kind of preposterous experience. The way she treated me was completely unfair. Up to that moment, it had been such a pleasant, tranquil spring evening. But strangely enough, I couldn't work up any anger. For the moment, a wave of bewilderment and confusion swept over me, swept any sense of logic away.

WHEN I GOT TO THE TOP of the stairs and out of the building, it was no longer spring, and the moon had disappeared from the sky. This was no longer the street I knew. I'd never before seen the trees lining the street. Thick, slimy snakes wound themselves tightly around the trunks, like wriggling living ornaments. Their scales rustled drily as they rubbed against the bark. The sidewalk was ankle deep in whitish ash, and there were faceless men and women walking along, exhaling a yellowish, sulfurous breath from deep within their throats. The air was bitterly cold, almost freezing. I turned up the collar of my suit.

"You should be ashamed of yourself," the woman said.

A NOTE ABOUT THE AUTHOR

Haruki Murakami was born in Kyoto in 1949 and now lives near Tokyo. His work has been translated into more than fifty languages, and the most recent of his many international honors is the Hans Christian Andersen Literature Award, whose previous recipients include Karl Ove Knausgård, Isabel Allende, and Salman Rushdie.

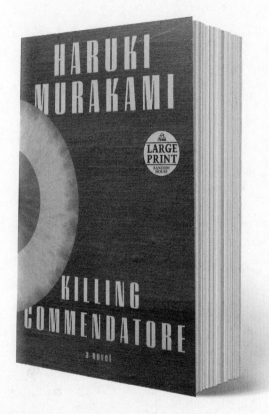